A TRAIL OF JEWELS

D.C. Moore

The characters and events portrayed in this book are fictitious. Any similarity to real persons, living or dead, is coincidental and not intended by the author.

ISBN-13: 9798857504703

Cover design by: D.C. Moore & B. West
Printed in the United States of America

For Alex. For always sticking with me.

CONTENTS

1

"Hurry children." His father said, fixing his navy jacket as the guards led them down the dark hallway. The boy had fallen a few steps behind his youngest sister, who had taken notice and stopped to grab his hand.

The boy was the youngest of five children. His youngest sister was a few years older than he, which is why they had always been close. His older sisters always had a charm of protecting him, but not as closely as she had.

Firmly grabbing his hand, the youngest sister smiled at him and pulled him forward, almost causing the young boy to miss a step as they continued down the darkened hall.

They were moved to this location recently by another set of guards during the ongoing war. The boy's family had been moved around quite a bit in the last nine months, and he was never sure why. At only thirteen years old, the boy speculated with his older sisters about what might be going on outside the doors of their imprisonment but could never seem to get an answer from anyone.

"Come along." His youngest sister said in a hushed tone. The boy smiled briefly at her before noticing a guard looking directly at them. Immediately, the boy refocused his gaze toward the end of the hall, where a solid wooden door awaited them.

Thinking about the last few months, the boy remembered the place where they were before this decrepit building; a much bigger residence about two hours away with his sisters and parents, where they had been for months. They spent most of their time writing friends who resided back home, knowing that they would rarely get a response. His eldest sister wrote the most, always hoping and praying for a reply of good hope, but none ever came.

After a while, the guards came for his mother and father, taking them away to their residence, but leaving him and his sisters behind for another month. For what seemed like ages, the boy remained at the seemingly abandoned home, surrounded by guards. His sisters continued writing but he couldn't think of anyone to write to, so instead he created a journal, logging his entries daily. After some time, loneliness set in, making him feel even more isolated than he had felt before.

Occasionally he and his sisters would attempt to peer out of the window. They could always see the guards at their stations, pacing back and forth and peering into the home. Sometimes they saw people walking down the street, normal civilians with normal lives, very much unlike themselves. They would look out of the window until they were spotted by a guard, who would usually come in and reprimand them. The guards didn't seem to be hateful most of the time, but there were a few that did not take well to him and his sisters, berating them for the simplest of tasks like sitting too close to a window, or looking strangely at them.

Another tug at the boy's hand made him realize that he had fallen behind again. His youngest sister gave a disappointing nod as he took a couple of quick steps to catch up. They had reached the door.

The guard grabbed the brass knob on the door and twisted

it, revealing a stairwell that led into a basement. The boy peered at his mother, who looked just as stone-faced as she had been the last few months. He remembered when he was younger, she was much softer but had always been protective of him. Knowing that he was the only son of five children, his mother had taken extra care of him to ensure his safety. She was always the one telling him when he couldn't do something, and he often listened.

His father on the other hand, was quite the opposite. He would encourage the boy to do more adventurous things such as horseback riding or boating. But that ended a couple years ago when the boy fell off a boat and injured himself severely. His mother thought he wouldn't survive the fall. Luckily, after a few weeks of pain and misery, the boy did indeed survive, but his mother kept an even more stern eye on him.

Following his family, the boy took the first step down the stone stairs. Below, he could see a few dimmed lights that seemed to flicker on and off. The smell of musty dust filled his nostrils, and he began to feel lightheaded.

His father had told them they needed to be dressed appropriately, as they would be moving to their next location soon. The boy made sure to put on his best jacket and pants, adorned with his favorite hat. His sisters had spent months mending his clothing, sewing beautiful jewels and stones into it. The boy often questioned why the stones were being put on the inside of the jacket instead of the outside where they could be seen, but his sisters simply responded that they were there to guide and protect, not to show off. He didn't know what they meant by that comment but was excited to wear the outfit his sisters had tailored for him, even if it was a bit heavier.

The beams of light from behind him began to dampen as the wooden door closed, the slam startling his younger sister. She gripped his hand even tighter. He looked at her again and smiled as they descended the next step.

"You are okay?" He nodded at her question, and she nodded in return. The boy could tell that something hadn't felt right since they left their room that evening but couldn't quite figure out what. A sense of dread crept down his neck the closer they got to their destination.

His oldest sister walked behind his mother, almost as stone-faced as she had been. The time in solitude the last few months had put a damper on her demeanor. A look of hopelessness adorned his oldest sister's face, shrouded by her chestnut blonde hair. Her pure white dress shimmered in the faint lights that trickled down the stairwell. She had always been a younger version of his mother, and sometimes just as protective. These last few months had aged her greatly, now starting to resemble their mother even more than before.

Another door stood at the bottom of the stairwell, this time wide open. Looking ahead, the boy could see a few chairs sitting in the middle of an empty room, but not enough for all of them to use. Counting the people around him being led into the room there were eleven, but only four chairs.

The boy squeezed his sister's hand again, this time feeling more worried than before. His sister squeezed back, echoing the same worry as he looked at her face.

Once down the stairs, the room appeared much more spacious, but a room was all it was. There were no markings on the walls, a few lights to illuminate the space, and no other door or window to the outside world besides the one that they had just entered through, which the boy could feel closing behind him as the wind brushed against his back.

"What is this?" his father asked as he turned towards one of the guards. His brown beard had grown a little longer in the last few months, now edging past the small point on his chin and dangling a little further down his neckline. His mustache still appeared well groomed as it curled out on either side, extending away from the rest of his facial hair. A few gray flecks had started to appear in his beard and on top of his head. His father had also aged greatly in these last few months.

One of the guards looked at him with an expressionless face before responding. "Please sit and wait." The guard then turned around and walked back towards the door. His father hung his head before looking at his mother, who remained cold as stone.

The four chairs became occupied quickly, sitting his father, mother, oldest sister, and himself. His three younger sisters stood behind him, his youngest sister directly behind, still grabbing onto his hand. Also behind them were a few other members of their household, people who had been with them for a very long time and had been loyal to the family for as long as the boy could remember. Their facial expressions echoed the same sentiment of worry as the others.

The door opened again revealing another guard, who appeared to be more decorated than the rest, adorning medals and a few ribbons on the lapel of his jacket. In his hand was a small piece of paper, about the size of a postcard.

Before the door closed, the man stood in front of them, four guards on each side, and he began to raise the paper toward his face. Each guard had their hands on their holstered weapons, seemingly waiting for one of his family members to make a move. The boy grew even more anxious, a feeling of terror beginning to slip into his mind.

The man began reading the paper after stating his father's name aloud. "Given the fact..."

Suddenly, the boy's ears started ringing. The noise drowned out the rest of the sentence, but he knew what it meant. His family had been held hostage for months, taken to secure locations, and now, they were here to live out their final moments together before a firing squad.

Once again, his sister gripped his hand tightly. She had come to the same realization. The ringing in his ears began to dull his hearing as he could hear his second oldest sister start to sob.

His father turned to his family, then back toward the medaled man, attempting to make a plea. "What? What!?" But a chance to plea was not granted.

The guards unholstered their guns and aimed.

A barrage of loud bangs sounded as pain shot through his rib. The screams of his family erupted into his eardrums. He tried once more to look at his youngest sister, her grip loosening on his hand. He felt her hand slip away as he collapsed onto the floor. In an instant, the world went black.

2

His head was still throbbing, his muscles ached, and his ribs felt as if they were broken. He could feel discomfort in his leg but not enough to drown out the pain he felt everywhere else. He kept his eyes clenched shut, afraid of what he might see if he opened them. There was some type of weight being forced on his right side, as if something had been laid across him. Around him, he could hear a motor running somewhere around him and the sound of rainfall pelting some type of canvas material.

Finally, after a few moments of dread, the boy slowly opened his left eye. Darkness shrouded his view as he attempted to take in his surroundings. He tried to move his head to get an idea of where he might be. Above him, the rain continued pelting the canvas of what seemed like some type of truck or other large vehicle. To his right lay his youngest sister, silent and motionless as blood seeped from her mouth and pooled into the boy's jacket.

He tried to keep himself from screaming, throwing his left

hand over his mouth. Before him, his youngest sister's corpse, and around him, the rest of his family lay still, all of them dead.

The boy gasped lightly, attempting to hold back sobs. If the guards had found out he was still alive, they would surely make haste at finishing the job. Here he was in a mound of his massacred family, but he had no time to mourn. He had to find a way to escape.

Tilting his head up, he could hear two guards talking in the front of the truck, the rain still pounding on the canvas of the truck bed.

"Where are we taking them?" One guard asked in an extremely deep voice. The boy recognized the voice as someone who had guarded them at the previous home where they were held captive. He believed him to be one of the nice ones but was seemingly proven wrong.

"Outside of town, deep in the woods. We are to bury the bodies in a mine and disfigure them as much as possible." The other guard's voice seemed much higher, but more commanding. The deep-toned guard's silent response seemed to concern the other, causing the commanding guard to pose a question. "Why? Second thoughts?"

"No, sir. Just curious." Afterward, the silence returned, now filled again with the purring of the motor and the rain coming down.

Looking down at his feet, the boy could see a sliver of an opening as the flap to the canvas waved in the wind. He could still hear a faint ringing in his ears. Outside, he could see another truck following close behind. He wondered how he was going to escape.

Taking another deep breath, he brought his left hand up to his chest, pushing on his sister's body to nudge her out of the way. The boy maneuvered back and forth a few times before finally feeling his sister's body give way to his freedom. Her lifeless body slumped down, planting her face into the stomach of another body, but the boy could not be sure who.

Now having a better view of his surroundings, the boy

looked to see who might be in the car with him. On the furthest end of the cab, he noticed a hand that was neatly decorated with rings and a diamond bracelet that belonged to his mother. Lying next to his sister was a pale-faced man, eyes open and mouth agape as if in shock. He flinched when he recognized it was the body of his father.

He tried to shake off his thoughts, pushing his body towards the back of the cab where the canvas was flapping vigorously. He could still hear the guards in the front of the truck making small talk, but he tried once more to focus only on escaping. Peering at the headlights behind them, he wondered how many guards or soldiers were in the truck. How many had been sent to ensure that they were properly disposed of? How many could still be coming?

The revolution had taken quite a toll on thousands of lives. The boy had imagined many of the people he knew had been killed on the battlefield or by the same soldiers that led him and his family to their graves. How many lives had been lost? How many more to come?

Thoughts raced through his mind as the truck stopped abruptly, causing him to grab onto one of the ledges of the bed of the truck. Outside, he could hear another man talking in the distance as the truck came to a complete stop.

"Can I help you boys?" An older man's voice called out.

"Just out to check the local areas." The first guard stated. "Seen anything we need to be aware of?"

The doors of the truck behind the vehicle he was in opened simultaneously, followed by the sound of them closing again and footsteps approaching. The boy hunkered back into the truck bed, readying himself to lay flat and play dead if the canvas moved even slightly. Instead, the guard's footsteps moved past, towards the front where the old man continued speaking to the guards.

This was the moment of opportunity. He wasn't sure if there were other vehicles behind the other truck, but he knew there wasn't time to find out. Clutching his side in pain as he lunged forward, he poked his head out of the canvas to look around. There didn't appear to be anyone else within his eyesight.

Positioning himself with one leg out of the truck, the boy moved to ease himself completely onto the muddy ground. His feet hit the ground at the same time, and, for a moment, he stopped to make sure the guards did not hear him. Ahead, he could still hear them talking civilly to the old man at the front of the caravan.

Peering around the back of the truck, the boy could see all the guards' backs were facing him. To the left of the truck sat a wooded area that extended far beyond his line of sight. At that moment, the boy darted into the woods, bracing himself against any of the trees he could get his hands on. The intense pain in his ribs subsided as adrenaline flowed through his body. He didn't have time to think or cry, only to run.

Finding shelter behind a large tree, the boy kneeled on the ground and peered back toward the trucks. The two guards returned to their truck as the old man stepped aside, permitting them to continue onward, with the bodies of the boy's family still in the truck bed. The old man waved as they drove by, his white stained shirt seemingly soaked from the rain and his brown trousers caked in mud from the walk. He looked like he'd been outside for quite some time in the rain.

Suddenly, the old man turned his head, making eye contact with the boy in the woods.

The boy's eyes grew wide. Without thinking, he immediately turned around and ran deeper into the woods. The pain in his ribs returned, burning like hellfire, but he couldn't stop. Surely the old man would alert the guards if he had the chance.

He had to survive, someway, somehow. So, he ran.

3

Clutching his side, the boy ran further into the woods. He wasn't sure if the guards heard him make his escape, but he didn't want to take the time to find out. He pushed himself to keep running deeper into the woods, praying that his footsteps were light enough to keep the guards from noticing.

After a few minutes, he stopped and positioned his body behind a tree. His ribs roared in pain as he kept his right hand pressed against them. Taking three deep breaths in succession, he peered his head around to see if the guards and the trucks were still there. They appeared to be moving further out of sight, which made him breathe a sigh of relief.

Questions rushed through his brain as he tried to maintain his focus. Where were they taking his family? How long until they noticed he was missing? Would they come back to find him? The images of his family's corpses began penetrating his brain. So many lives were lost, he didn't want to be counted among them.

Slowly, he moved his hands toward his neck, removing

a few buttons on his coat. Underneath lay another long shirt followed by bare skin; jewels in the coat rubbing the area where his ribs felt raw. A bullet must have struck him there during the massacre of his family but had not managed to fully get through. The jewels had protected him but did not provide the same protection for his four sisters, who had also sewn jewels into their own clothing. For a moment, he felt grateful to be alive.

Letting out another sigh, the boy turned around and rested his head against the trunk of the tree. He pondered what to do next, thinking about the possibility of finding the forces of men that his father had worked with. Surely they would be able to help him unless they were dead or compromised. He wasn't sure whom to trust because those he did trust were most likely on their way to a shallow grave.

Beads of sweat began to drip from his head and down his cheek. The July heat combined with the heavy military jacket he was wearing made him realize he was overheating. He pulled again at another few buttons, revealing more of the white undershirt and noticing the small red blotches poking through. He was bleeding, but only a little. In his case though, a little bit of blood could mean a lot of harm. He thought about his mother for a moment. She had told him when he was little, he had a bleeding disease, one with no cure but was highly treatable. A tiny cut could mean months of bed rest.

He wanted to cry, to weep at the loss of his family. Everyone close to him had been murdered, betrayed by a people whose very foundation was built by his own family's blood, sweat, and tears. He had always been taught to be humble, to think carefully before speaking, and to give the benefit of the doubt whenever possible. His mother had tried to instill these values early in him, but all he could feel was anger, hatred, and sorrow.

Tears began falling from his eyes, mixing with the sweat that still poured from his forehead. Staying still, the boy allowed his tears to touch his lips, his tongue grazing the salty liquid. He clenched his eyes, attempting to cease the flow of tears, but it seemed to only make it worse. For a moment, he let himself go, giving in to the sadness of his loss.

A sudden crunching noise alerted him, and his sobs immediately ceased. Someone was approaching, the crunching noise moving closer to the tree. He didn't know what to do. If he ran, surely the person would shoot, and his jewels would only protect the front half of his body.

Thinking about the jewels made him realize he had unbuttoned his coat, revealing his open chest. He scrambled to button them back up as fast as he could, the footsteps now within feet of where he was hiding.

A few passing seconds felt like hours. The steps got closer and closer until he felt like they were standing right on top of him. He clenched his eyes shut, praying that whatever happened next happened quickly.

"You lost, boy?" A man's voice he had head before rang in his ears. Still, he hesitated to look up at the man, afraid of what he might see if he did. "I said, are you lost?" The boy still didn't answer. Instead, he shook his head from left to right, hoping the man would turn away and leave him be.

Forcing his head up, he looked to see the older man from earlier staring down at him, his white stained undershirt and walking stick visible through the light rain droplets that hit his head. "I saw you flee that convoy there." Immediately, the boy clenched in fear, grasping the idea that this might be the end. "Are you alone?"

The boy nodded in affirmation. An uneasy feeling still shrouded the area. He wouldn't allow himself to speak for fear of giving himself away.

"That is a shame..." The old man stated in an almost morose tone. Suddenly, he felt a hand grab his arm and began pulling him up to his feet. "Come on now, let's get you somewhere dry. This rain isn't going to do anything but make you sick." The rain had almost ceased by now, reduced to a simple mist.

Rising to his feet, he stared at the old man as he fumbled

with his walking stick. He wasn't sure why the man would be helping him, but it seemed to be the only refuge he was going to find, so he followed close behind him.

Slow footsteps in another direction, not toward the convoy, but further to the west. The boy breathed heavily as he adjusted his jacket, the jewels still piercing into his ribs, causing him to occasionally grunt in pain.

The man stopped suddenly and turned to face him. "Uncomfortable?" He couldn't tell if he was talking about the jacket or just general concern. "Hmm...maybe if you take the jacket off and cover your head, that might help." He raised his head toward the sky, and the boy mimicked his movements, feeling the droplets hit his face. "Seems like it's just going to get worse tonight."

After a second thought, the boy began to unbutton the jacket, revealing once again the white shirt stained with a patch of blood that had doubled in size since they started walking, now moving down his torso. Slipping the jacket off, he flung it over his head and shoulders, the jewels clanging against his clavicle as they landed. The rain pelting the jacket harder as he took another breath.

"We had better keep going." The man announced, looking in the direction in which he was walking. "If they find that you're not there, you know they'll come looking for you."

No audible response, but an unseen nod came from the boy as he trotted behind the man. The forest appeared to get denser the further they walked. It felt like they walked for hours in silence, occasionally stopping for the man to catch a quick breath before continuing.

Finally, a small light appeared in the distance. The boy wondered what could be up ahead. As they got closer, he noticed the light was coming from a small window in a cottage. The wooden cottage was surrounded by darkness, but his eyes had adjusted to make out a small buggy and horse barn to the left. Both buildings appeared to be in disrepair.

As they approached, the boy could make out another

figure inside the house. Suddenly, his fears began to grow, and he thought about running again. Looking down at his shirt, he noticed the red spot now covered the majority of the front. He was surprised that he wasn't feeling queasy or uneasy as he usually did when he got any type of scrape.

The front door appeared just as raggedy as the rest of the cottage, the rotting boards showing on the face with a big bronze handle to keep the door closed. The man grabbed for the handle and pushed down, allowing the light from inside to illuminate him, revealing a scar on the left side of the man's face. The boy wanted to question him about it but thought twice and remained silent.

"You're finally home." An elderly woman's voice said from inside. "Leave those boots outside, they have to be filthy." Her accent seemed deeper than that of the old man.

Turning around to the boy, the man nodded. "You heard the misses." Looking down, the boy could see that his boots were caked in layers of mud from the walk. Putting his foot on the opposite boot, he pried the first off. The second boot seemed a little more difficult, as he tried not to touch the mud with his sock but could barely bend down without causing pain to his ribs. Finally, the boot relented and fell to the ground. The man already had his boots off and was inside.

The woman's voice bellowed again. "Close the door, Luka. I don't want any of the rain getting in here." Luka, the man, motioned for the boy to come inside. The boy nodded and stepped through the wooden frame into the small cottage.

Inside, a table sat against the window which adorned a small candle on the sill, and a couple of chairs surrounding it. A tiny, dark room in the back appeared to be some type of washroom. A small wooden ladder jutted from the edge of the kitchen to a loft with a bed. Everything seemed to be accessible through the main area, which appeared very convenient. To the right, another door remained shut, leaving its contents unknown.

The older woman came into view as she appeared from

the washroom, her plain gray skirt falling to her feet and a gray buttoned shirt to match. Her hair was mostly silver, with strands of brown still holding on from her younger years.

"I didn't realize that you would be gone so long at the..." Suddenly, she realized the boy was standing next to Luka and she let out an audible gasp.

"Luka..." She covered her mouth as she slowly approached. The boy grew tense again, for fear of what the woman might do. "Do you know..."

"Yes, Klara." Luka responded before Klara could finish her sentence. "And the boy needs our help. Let's...leave it at that for now."

Lowering her hand, Klara's face became warm. "Yes, indeed he does." She approached the boy and put out her hand. "May I?" The boy looked at her as she motioned for the jacket, which was still covering his head and shoulders. He removed the jacket and flinched before handing it over to her. She was taken aback at the sheer weight of it but hadn't realized the inside had been lined with jewels. She placed the jacket on one of the wooden chairs and turned back to face him. "Come, let's get you cleaned up." She looked down at his ribs, the blood now starting to leak into his suit pants. "And let's take care of that wound." Luka nodded in his direction, giving the boy the okay to follow Klara to the washroom.

Klara sat him down and asked him to remove his shirt, which he obliged. She flinched at the sight of the small gash on his side, wondering why so much blood had poured out of a small wound.

"May I?" She asked again, this time for permission to clean the wound. The boy nodded. A few minutes of grunting and clenching caused the boy to feel faint as Klara wiped down the wound and applied a small bandage, wrapping a cloth around his whole body to secure it tightly. She took another damp cloth from the washbasin and wiped the boy's forehead and cheeks, the warm water felt good against his skin. "There." She said, as she put the cloth back beside the washbasin. Her concerned look followed from the boy's face over to Luka, who was now sitting in the other kitchen chair. "How did you find him? What about..."

Luka took a deep breath. "The others...are not so lucky, I'm afraid." The boy could see that Luka had pulled out a pocketknife and was whittling at a piece of wood. "I was stopped by a convoy of soldiers earlier this evening. They had asked about my whereabouts, and I asked the same. They were much more reluctant than I, but that's how I saw the young man escape."

The boy paused for a second as Luka referred to him as 'man'. In all his thirteen years, he had never been referred to as a 'man'. Instead, his titles had always been a bit more noble. He found it intriguing that Luka called him 'boy' in private but 'man' in front of Klara. He had always seen himself as a boy, until tonight.

She looked down at him again and stared into his eyes. Her eyes were almost as gray as her clothes but appeared bright and full of hope. The boy didn't think he could say the same for himself. "Are they all..."

The boy nodded as Luka interjected. "I would assume so." A shred of wood fell to the floor as he put down the pocketknife and took a deep breath.

Klara shook her head in disbelief. "The whole world will turn upside down."

"It already has." Luka said staring out of the window, his gray hair prominent in the candlelight.

Although the boy had just learned both of their names, he was certain they already knew who he was, so there was no point in announcing it. Regardless, they seemed hard-pressed to assist him. Luka had aided in his escape and Klara didn't think twice when she recognized him that evening. For once in a very long while, the boy felt safe.

A noise came from outside. Something started scratching on the door. The boy felt uneasy again as his chest began to tighten. Luka rose from his seat and made his way over to the door, opening it slowly. The fear that they had already found him caused his breathing to become shorter as Klara took note of his state, placing a hand on his shoulder to calm him.

As Luka opened the door, a gray-haired animal appeared in the doorway. The dog shuffled his way inside, shaking his fur from the rain as Luka closed the door behind him.

"I was wondering where you had gone off to, Shep." Luka said as he patted his head. Immediately, the dog noticed the boy sitting in the washroom. Intrigued, he approached the boy, sniffing his knee, and analyzing his scent. The dog took one more sniff of the boy's hand, and then nuzzled it, allowing the boy to move his hand down Shep's head, causing the dog's tongue to stick out and appearing to grin.

The boy smiled for the first time in what seemed like years.

4

A beam of light shined through the cabin window as the boy opened his eyes. Chirping birds could be seen flying outside in the woods. Around him, a shroud of blankets surrounded his body, encasing him in a cocoon of warmth. Downstairs he could hear the old woman, Klara, humming as some dishes clanged against the wooden countertop, and the smell of tomato soup and fresh bread coursed through his nostrils.

The night had been stressful, and the boy could barely believe he had slept a wink. Yet, with the stress of the evening, his body had forced itself to shut down. After Klara had assisted in cleaning his wound, the boy was escorted up the ladder to the bed in the loft. As he lay there, all he could think about was his family and the fact that he would never see them again. His mother's soft voice echoed in his ear. His father's stern, general-like demeanor stuck in his vision. His sisters, all their laughter and voices were now overshadowed by the last thing he had heard from them, their screams. Tears began to fall from his eyes as he lay there, thinking about how everything had happened over the last few months and the fact that he knew he still wasn't anywhere close to being safe.

He pondered for a moment what the old man, Luka, and Klara might do. Luka was the one who saved him last night. If it weren't for him, surely the guards would have noticed and found him by now, intending to finish the job they had started. On the other hand, Luka might try to profit and use him as leverage against the uprising, staging a hefty ransom for his return. He quickly wrote this thought off as it didn't seem to make sense. Ultimately, the boy felt he could trust these two, the farmer and his wife. In the last twelve hours, they had done nothing but protect and care for him. He wondered if one day he might be able to return the favor. If he lived long enough to see it, that is.

A motion at the foot of the bed startled him. He lifted his head above the blanket to the couple's dog, Shep, still sleeping at the edge of the mattress. Another small smile ran across his face as he peered at the European Shepard.

He wondered what time it was. How long had he been asleep? The boy stretched his arms above his head, causing a twinge of pain in his side. He had forgotten about the wound. The jewels had only grazed his side, but it was just enough to send the area pooling with blood, staining his white undershirt and jacket. Now he was adorned in another white undershirt, but one that was too big, and the pair of his own trousers.

Shuffling the blanket out of the way, he noticed that Shep was startled awake from the motion. The boy looked at him fondly as he did in return, and then laid his head back down on the pillow, ears still perked.

Shifting his feet from under the covers, the boy planted his feet on the wooden floor of the loft. A slight creaking had erupted from the floorboards below as he stood up as far as he could without hitting the ceiling.

"Sounds like someone is awake." He heard Klara's voice from downstairs. The boy didn't respond audibly but instead made his way over to the ladder and down the stairs to the main floor.

Upon reaching the ground, the boy planted both socked feet onto the wooden slats of the cabin. Looking up, Shep had now taken a four-legged stance on the bed before peering back down at him.

The tomato smell filled the cabin as the boy looked over at the stove. A pot of soup sat simmering as Klara removed a fresh loaf of bread from the oven. Both components were still powered by wood, something the boy hadn't seen in his lifetime. Mostly everything in his life had been powered by electricity up to this point.

Klara had on an apron over her gray dress, the same dress as yesterday. He had never seen someone so decked out in grey before, but it seemed fitting for Klara as she turned around to look at him. Her face scrunched a little as she observed him standing there.

"You'd better wash your face before breakfast." She pointed in the direction of the washroom as she sat the bread on the stove. "Luka will be back any minute now."

At that moment, the boy's hesitancy returned. Where could Luka have gone? To get the guards? The Generals? Anxiety filled his brain, and his palms began to sweat. The thought of being captured again made him seize in terror. He thought about bursting through the front door of the cabin, making a run for the woods, but he couldn't force his body to budge. Instead, he stood there like a stone. His mind played all the possible outcomes.

Suddenly, he could feel a hand on his shoulder. His eyes refocused on Klara as she stared at him, seemingly worried. "Child, we are not meant to harm you." Her calming voice sent a rush of relief through his spine. "Luka brought you here. We will protect you." The reassurance sent another wave of calm into him, his anxiety lowering. "We must." The last thing she said seemed peculiar, but it let the boy know one thing; they most certainly knew who he was.

"Now..." Klara uttered slightly under her breath. "Go wash up." She pointed to the washroom again, as if the boy had already forgotten the location inside the small cabin. Turning back around, she made her way back to the stove.

The boy sighed, mostly with relief, but also with a hint of concern. If the couple knew who he was, then that means they knew what had happened to his family. If others find out, it could lead to chaos, and he wasn't sure if he wanted to be around when another war started.

The washroom basin sat empty with a jug directly next to it. Not having running water in the home was also something the boy was not used to, but he figured he could make do. Grabbing the pitcher, he poured a little into the basin of the sink, allowing the water to pool two or three inches before stopping and placing the pitcher back down.

He submerged his hands into the water and brought them up to his face, the water felt refreshing against his skin as it dripped back into the sink. To the right, he grabbed a small hand cloth and began to wipe his face. The cloth was much rougher than what he was used to, but it would do the trick for now.

Directly in front of him he saw himself in the mirror. Strangely, he didn't even recognize himself at first. Some of his features seemed darker, and some seemed lighter. His cheeks were not as flush as they were before, and his forehead furrow seemed permanent. The boy he had seen yesterday morning was not the boy he was looking at today. Something inside him died last night, along with everyone he knew and loved. Now, standing before him was a shell of a dynasty, a mere semblance of what could have been. Was death the only option now?

Blinking, the boy brought himself back to reality. Drying his hands, he sat the cloth down on the counter of the washroom and walked out into the main area of the small wooden cabin.

Klara had set the modest kitchen table next to the window with two ceramic bowls and two spoons. Moving closer, the boy could see the steam rising from both bowls, indicating that she had already served the soup. He hesitated before moving closer to the table.

"Sit." The old woman said as she motioned her hand to the

chair. The boy obeyed, positioning himself to pull the seat out and sit down. He wasn't sure what to do next though. With his family, he would have to wait for everyone to be seated, served, then he could eat. The fact that Klara was not sitting with him made him feel uneasy. "You don't have to wait on me, dear. Please, go ahead. You must be starved."

Looking down at the bowl of tomato soup, a slice of bread sat beside it. The soup smelled delicious, probably the most enticing meal he'd had in a few months. Taking his right hand, he grabbed the bread and began to tear a piece with his left. Dunking the bread into the soup, he brought the piece to his lips before opening his mouth to ingest it. The smell and taste paralleled as the boy chewed his first bite of food in what felt like years. The second bite was the same, as was the third. The boy developed a fluid motion as he continued to tear bits of bread and dip into the soup.

Before he knew it, the whole bowl of soup and bread had disappeared. It was as if he had blocked out the whole event in his mind. He couldn't believe how hungry he was, and his stomach continued to growl for more soup.

A second bowl and some bread appeared in front of him as Klara cleared the first bowl from the table. The boy didn't hesitate, and the second bowl was gone just as quickly, if not quicker than the first.

"My goodness..." Klara stated as she looked back at him. "Well, I supposed you needed it. Would you like another?" The boy shook his head, declining a third bowl. Klara grinned.

Turning his focus to the window, the boy noticed the woods they had journeyed through the night before. This morning, they looked light and breezy, not having the same foreboding feeling as they had previously. Still, his nerves overtook him, feeling as if a soldier or a guard could just emerge from the shadows of the trees at any moment.

A shadow appeared at the edge of the forest and he feared his suspicions were correct, until he saw Luka emerge from the tree line with a satchel in his hand.

Shep must have heard Luka's footsteps as he jumped from the bed onto the floor of the cabin. The boy was seemingly impressed as that jump had to have been six or seven feet up, but the dog acted like it was a mere step. Shep made his way towards the door to greet Luka, but not before stopping by the boy's side, allowing him to receive a few pats on the head.

As the door opened, the boy noticed that his boots were no longer outside. He figured someone must have brought them inside so that no one would see them and figure out he was there. For a moment, the boy realized that the couple were putting themselves in harm's way to ensure his safety. A feeling of gratitude briefly swept over himself before Luka closed the door and laid the sack on the floor next to the table. A couple of fish heads protruded from the bag, causing the boy to grimace.

"How was the market?" Klara asked as Luka took off his hat. The old man sat down on the chair across from him.

"A little cold out this morning, but there were lots of people about." Luka took his bread and began to rip and dip, just as the boy had done a few minutes earlier. "No one seems to be none the wiser about the circumstances surrounding us though." He took a bite of his bread and continued speaking. "Which is to be expected I suppose. They've hid their presence for this long, what's another few days?" The boy realized that Luka was speaking about his family but declined to question him or add anything further.

Klara spoke up from behind him. "Surely the people will know soon enough." She grabbed his bowl and proceeded to lay down another piece of bread, this time with no soup to dip into. The boy began to tear the bread.

"I see you've gotten an appetite." Luka said as he peered over at him. The old man had a grin on his face, something he had not seen up until now, causing the boy to nod as he continued eating. "That's good." He nodded, taking a bite of his tomato-drenched bread. "But I do hope you know you won't be able to stay with us for long."

Suddenly, the boy's senses deepened, and his face went

cold. Of course he had to understand that he would not be able to seek refuge in this cabin forever, but he didn't realize that Luka would speak of it so soon. He was grateful for the generosity the couple had shown him over the last two days, but he wasn't quite sure where to go next, or who he could rely on.

"We can't just send him off into the wilderness, Luka." Klara intervened, her face becoming stern. As the boy's anxiety grew, his palms began to sweat again.

"No, we won't do that." Luka looked up at him, he could tell that the boy was stressed. "I have a friend in another town, someone who may be able to help us get you somewhere safe." He looked down for a moment. "Somewhere safer than here. This place is too close. They will surely find you here."

The thought of meeting someone else to take him to a different location caused a flashback. A family trip turned into a six-month string of events, never to return home. Perhaps this was the next journey, and home needed to be somewhere else this time around, wherever that might be.

"We must find a way to get you on a train. It's the only way to get you out of here." Luka sat back in his chair, seemingly pondering a plan in his head. "If I can get a couple of tickets for us, I can journey alongside you until we meet with my contact. I can let him know that we are coming and when to expect us. Then we can do a handoff at the train station. Of course, we'd need to find you some different clothes. Something that no one will recognize you in."

The boy sat there for a moment, perplexed that the old man had seemingly thought this whole thing through in just a few minutes being at the table.

Klara moved to the boy's side. "It's settled then." She placed her hand on the boy's shoulder once more. "Tomorrow you two will head into town for the train station. But for tonight, we stay here, and you stay inside." She looked down at the boy.

The boy nodded as Klara removed her hand from his shoulder, moving back to the kitchen area of the cabin. He was surprised by the amount of effort that these two had put into getting him safely to his next destination. But there was one thing on his mind which caused him to utter the first word that either of the couple had heard from him.

"Why?" The boy asked hesitantly. "Why help us? Why help me?" He looked at them both as they hung their heads.

Luka sat for a moment before lifting his head to respond. "Because we believe in you."

5

The day went by much quicker than the boy had anticipated. As Luka went back to town to get in touch with his contact, the boy helped Klara with cleaning up around the cabin. Early in the afternoon, she tended to his wound again, changing the bandages and remarking that it seemed to look better than it had before. The boy found that hard to believe considering his experience with his previous injuries, but smirked at her when she looked up at him.

For a small cabin, there was a lot of cleaning that needed to be done. He took charge of the loft area and the washroom, seeing as those had been the two places where he had spent the most time since he arrived. Making the bed in the loft made him wonder where the couple had slept that night, and where they would sleep tonight, knowing there would be no way they would let him sleep anywhere but the loft. He figured that they made themselves comfortable in the couple of rocking chairs directly below the loft in an alcove behind the washroom.

His mother had always cared so deeply for him and his

sisters and guarding them with her life. He thought about what his mother would say if she were there, would she be happy that he had escaped, or fearful of his future? A tear fell from his cheek as he wiped his face with his hand. He was sure Klara had taken notice, but she did not say anything and instead continued scrubbing the kitchen floor.

Later that evening, Luka had made his way back from town with another satchel on his back. This time the satchel contained clothes for the boy. A black flat cap to hide his face, a blue jacket with side buttons like the one he wore when he arrived, a baggy white buttoned shirt, a green vest, black trousers, and black boots. The boy sifted through the clothes, wondering if this plan would even work.

"The blue jacket is for after we get on the train. The rest you'll wear to the train station tomorrow." Luka explained to him. As he tried on the clothes, everything seemed a little baggy to his liking, except for the trousers. Klara was quick at attempting to fix it, but Luka stopped her. "He must not look his finest, dearest. Please remember." This caused her to pause momentarily before grabbing at the white buttoned shirt again.

"Regardless, he doesn't need to look like a vagrant." She exclaimed. Klara spent about an hour fixing the shirt as Luka reheated the tomato soup and bread for dinner. She made the boy try on the shirt just to make sure it fit him better, which it did. A change of clothes felt nice, and the boy was a little sad he couldn't just wear the outfit immediately.

After dinner, the couple settled down in their rocking chairs with Shep at Luka's feet. The boy sat on the floor, staring at the empty fireplace in front of him. The weather was too warm for a fire, and the ground had started to dry from the heavy rains the night before. Still, another world felt like it was inside that fireplace. A chute to the outside world. Who knows where he will end up next?

He remembered a time when his family had journeyed to Paris to see relatives and join in a celebration. The boy was much younger at the time, but he could still recall the elegant balls that took place while his family danced in the center as if the party had been thrown for them. His youngest sister would attempt to pull him onto the dance floor, but the boy had no interest in dancing. Still, he watched on with sheer fascination at the glittering gowns and dresses that were before him. The men in their fancy suits sporting women on their sides, swinging them around as if they were ragdolls. Things that the boy remembered now seemed to fade away in obscurity.

More tears started to fall from his face, this time knowing full well that Klara and Luka would take notice. At this point, he couldn't hold back any longer. The sobs started to bellow in his chest as he felt himself completely letting go.

The realization that he would never see his family again had finally hit. Those bodies that he gazed upon just yesterday, were those of the people he had spent all his life with, and now they were gone. The life that he had become accustomed to was over and his namesake ripped away.

Suddenly, he felt a presence surround him as if enveloped in a hug. Stopping briefly to look up, Klara had wrapped her arms around him, comforting him as she held back tears. The sobbing continued for a few more minutes before the boy could collect himself. Klara stayed there the whole time while Luka gazed off in the distance.

They had believed in him, believed in his family. He knew that there must be others out there who felt the same way. For that, he was grateful, but he wasn't sure how much good it would do.

Anxiety set in when it was time to lay his head down on the pillow that evening. All the boy could think about was the journey ahead, and what it meant for the future of his legacy. This was the first time he had felt extremely out of his comfort zone. Thrust into a world unlike any he had ever lived before. He would be fourteen in just a few short weeks, but the last few days seemed to age him more than a few years.

Adjusting his side to lay away from the bandage, he noticed the wound was slightly less painful than it had been earlier in the day. Klara had done a wonderful job of taking care of him during his short stay, and he was more than grateful to her. In just a twenty-four-hour span, she had already grown into another mother figure for him, and now he realized that he would be abandoning her as well in the morning. This thought caused a slight tinge of anger as he rustled in the blanket, attempting to make himself comfortable. Everyone he had ever known would be dead or absent from his life by this time tomorrow. Luka would travel with him on the train to the destination, then leave him with another stranger.

Letting his eyes settle on Shep, who was once again at the foot of the bed, he attempted to let his mind wander off into sleep. It was only an hour later he realized that he had just been staring at the dog and had not been asleep.

Lying on his back, the boy breathed deeply. He wondered if he would ever make it out of this place. Would he ever feel safe again, or is perpetual fear just something he would have to live with from now on?

His wandering mind caused him to eventually drift off into dreamland, where he saw his mother. She was standing on the edge of a cliff, beckoning him to come closer. The boy agreed, making his way towards her. All that he wanted was to feel her embrace once more. As he approached, her appearance turned dark, as did the world around him. He blinked and found himself in a dark room with his entire family, the same room he had been in just a little over a day ago. The cries of his family, pleading for their life, screaming for mercy echoed in his ears as shots rang out overhead. He tried to look around for any sign of them, but their screams were all that remained. Now the boy stood in a dark room by himself, the faint echoes of his family's slaughter reverberating through his eardrums. The dark room isolated him from everyone else. He felt alone and helpless and started to cry again.

Opening his eyes, he could see the sunrise beaming in through the cabin window. Tears stained the pillowcase as he wiped his eyes free from anything remaining. He wondered if the couple heard his sobs in the middle of the night.

Before departing that morning, the boy dressed himself in the outfit Luka had provided him. The buttoned white shirt fit much better than it had yesterday, thanks to Klara, and the green vest made him feel more like a normal person as he slipped it on. The trousers and boots fit a little looser than he cared to admit, but he felt that he didn't have a place to complain about ill-fitting clothes.

Luka handed the boy an empty leather satchel. The boy looked slightly confused in return.

"You'll need this for your trip." Luka exclaimed, walking over to the door to put on his boots. "It is yours from here on out." The boy nodded before audibly replying.

"Thank you." It felt strange to talk again. After speaking last night for the first time in a while, words somehow felt foreign to him, as if every time he was speaking it was in another language.

Klara walked up behind him, opening his leather satchel, and placing an entire loaf of bread inside. "I know you will get hungry, and considering how much bread you ate yesterday, you must have enjoyed it." She grinned. The boy nodded again with a slight smile in return, trying to force out another offer of thanks, but this time no words came out.

Placing the flat cap on his head, he walked over to the door. Luka was waiting as he turned back around to see the old woman one last time. Her grey hair shimmered in the sunlight in line with her grey dress.

Before he knew it, the boy had wrapped his arms around Klara, not from sorrow, but from a feeling of gratefulness.

"I am grateful for your generosity and hospitality." The boy said strongly. "One day, I will repay you." For a moment, he felt like himself again.

6

The small town closest to the couple's home did not have a train station, so Luka had to take the boy to the next town over which was about an hour away. Most of the journey was through the same woods that the boy had escaped through a couple of nights before, but he tried not to think about it as they walked along the paths toward the town.

Looking above him the sky seemed overcast, as if another rain shower might pummel them on their trek. Luka paid the sky no attention and instead kept his eyes on their destination. The boy never lingered, keeping directly behind Luka while still trying to remain silent.

"When we arrive, you'll need to keep your head down." Luka said in a sharp tone. "We don't want anyone to recognize you." The boy nodded in acknowledgment. His face would be his most recognizable feature, so he had to make sure the flat cap covered most of it. He practiced a bit during the walk by attempting to keep his head down while he took steps behind Luka, looking at the ground instead of the sky. It turned out to be much more difficult than he imagined it would be. His eyes kept wanting to focus forward, to look for any signs of danger, but he had to force himself to look down at the grass and branches that littered the ground below his feet.

After a little while longer, the town finally came into view. Luka adjusted the satchel on his back and turned to face the boy. "Stay close to me. No matter what happens, follow my direction. If I tell you to run, you run! Got it?" The old man's eyes were intense, causing the boy to only nod in agreement. "Good. We'll get you out of here, just stay calm and stay close."

The tree line broke right at the entrance of the town. Attempting to keep his head down, the boy tried to make out his surroundings. There seemed to be quite a few more people in this area than anywhere he had been in a long time. Staring at the peoples' feet who passed by, he noticed most of them were boots caked in multiple layers of mud. The pavement seemed cracked and old as if it needed repair. The boy kept his head down, forcing himself not to look up at what was in front of him besides Luka's boots.

"Large crowd ahead. Stay close." Luka muttered under his breath, just loud enough for the boy to hear him. He did as he was commanded and jutted up against Luka's back, as close as he could without touching him. His flat cap still shrouded his face in a shadow as he could hear voices becoming louder by the second. They were approaching the crowd, but why was there a crowd in the first place? He didn't have time to think as Luka turned sharply to the right, forcing the boy to notice only a moment later and follow suit.

The shouting of the crowd seemed muddled at first, rambling things he couldn't quite understand. As they drew closer, the noises morphed into actual words.

"Victory!"

"Freedom!"

"Revolution!"

The words seemed to reverberate through his ears. Keeping his eye on the pavement, the boy continued following close behind Luka's feet. The words the townspeople yelled were not in unison, just randomly being shouted by men at certain points. Everything else was just incoherent rambles.

As they made another turn, the pavement turned into cobblestone, before they passed through an iron gate. The change in scenery made the boy believe they were at the train station, or at least close to it. He could hear a locomotive engine not far in the distance.

Suddenly, Luka stopped, causing the boy to run right into his back. Luka only grunted before speaking.

"Two tickets, please." Luka said. He couldn't hear the location, only a piece of paper being opened and given to the attendant at the counter. For a moment, everything in front of him was quiet. Luka hadn't said a word which made the boy nervous, and the attendant did not respond immediately to Luka's request which heightened his concern.

Tilting his head to the left, he could see the crowd of people. A bunch of men in workman's clothes stood outside a bar, surrounding, and chatting with a man wearing a guard's uniform. The boy instantly felt sweat start to bead on his forehead, causing him to clench his eyes and put his head back down. He prayed that the guard did not see him. The guard didn't look or sound familiar, but he knew he would only remember the ones who watched over him while he was held captive with his family. He would not remember any new faces from the eve of his family's demise, nor would he recognize the voices.

"Your tickets, sir." The attendant at the counter finally said, slipping him two tickets as Luka handed over several rubles for payment.

"Thank you." Luka responded, turning around and placing his arm around the boy, attempting to guide him to the next destination. "We must get on this train as quickly as possible." The boy looked up at Luka, who seemed slightly concerned at the growing crowd outside the bar. He must have noticed the guard as well, maybe even recognizing him from the other night. Leading the boy to a bench, he motioned for him to sit, to which the boy obeyed.

"Stay here a moment. I'm going to see if we can board. Remember, keep your head down." The boy almost audibly responded but thought twice before nodding instead. With that, Luka walked toward the train cars.

The small town was bustling and picking up by the minute. Taking a slight look to the other side of the station, the boy could make out another large crowd beginning to form, this time outside of an old church. The war had made many people in the country nervous, and many of them had turned to religion to keep their minds focused. He couldn't blame them, as his family had done something similar, his mother becoming obsessed with religion right before they were all taken. Many of the men had gone off to fight, but older men stayed behind while others became guards. Everything started to feel a bit more unsettling as a third crowd began to form at the ticket line for the train.

The boy panicked again before thinking about what he could do next. Luka had informed him to stay, but if someone recognized him, that would be the end of it. If he tried to run, surely he'd be captured. If he stayed, someone might see him. He hoped that Luka would return soon.

A voice came from behind him, as if right next to his ear. "Poor little boy, all alone?" An elderly lady's voice crept into his eardrum, but the boy refused to respond, instead staying perfectly silent and still. His palms began sweating as he thought maybe if he remained silent, she'd go away.

But she didn't. "Little boys shouldn't be left alone in a place like this." He could hear her starting to make her way around toward his front. He kept his head down as her brown boots and dirty pleated skirt came into view. "Why don't you let me take you somewhere safe?" He still didn't respond, hoping that she would get the hint.

Suddenly, her hands were on his shoulders, shaking him back and forth. "No, you shouldn't be safe at all! Little vagrant boys should be fighting! Not running away! Why aren't you fighting!?" Her voice became raspy as the boy tried to clench his eyes shut. "You fight for victory! You fight for freedom! You fight for our Tsar! You..."

"That's enough!" Another voice bellowed a few feet away. It was Luka's voice. His boots appeared in front of him, grabbing his arm and pulling the boy toward him. "Leave this boy alone, he is not yours to hound, beggar woman."

The lady seemingly hissed at Luka. "A young, spry, boy should be fighting! Here, he is a waste of space, and I'd very much like to sell him at a high price." The boy nudged Luka, attempting to put distance between himself and the lady.

"You'll do no such thing." Luka snapped back. "Now, go away!" The lady hissed again before turning and walking in the opposite direction, her boots leaving a trail of mud behind. The boy let out a sigh of relief as Luka tugged on his vest to follow him. He didn't hesitate.

Approaching the train, Luka and the boy entered the second-to-last car and proceeded into one of the private rooms. Setting his satchel down, Luka stretched his arms for a moment, before instructing the boy to also place his satchel down.

"We're not out of the woods yet." Luka said, sitting down on one of the cushioned seats. "After the train departs, we'll need to hide you in the closet for a time. I'm the only one with an exit visa for our destination. You'll be safe so long as you stay hidden." At this point, the boy was beginning to feel like a piece of luggage, but he understood the concern.

"I will do as you command." The boy said with another nod. Luka grinned as he looked out the window. The crowd for the train line had grown immensely but it didn't appear like many were boarding the train, most were just sitting as soon as they left the ticket counter.

The train engine bellowed, and a sudden pull made the boy shift in his seat and his back hit the wall. They were beginning to move out of the station. Peering out one more time into the town, he saw the beggar woman, this time with her face looking around, possibly for another boy or girl to kidnap.

Her face looked aged, most likely fifty to sixty years old, but she seemed awfully spry for someone of that age. Her whole outfit had been caked in a muddy mess as if she had fallen into a pig pen.

Suddenly, the boy noticed something. Her eyes were locked on him, staring him down intently. He realized that his face was fully visible to the beggar, but it was too late now to make any sudden movements. Instead, he stared at her as she peered deeper into his soul, realizing who he was. Slowly, her arm raised, pointing her index finger in his direction as the train moved slightly faster. Her mouth hung agape as she fell out of eyesight. The boy breathed a sigh of relief again.

He hadn't forgotten his orders. As the train began moving faster, the boy crept inside the closet that was next to their seat. Luka nodded as he closed the door tightly, and it wasn't long before someone opened the private room door and requested to see Luka's exit visa, which he provided.

As the boy's eyes adjusted to the darkness, he felt another twinge of pain creep from the wound on his ribs. Praying that he had not ripped anything open, he looked down at his white buttoned shirt. No sign of blood came through the cloth that protected his wound. At some point he knew the bandage would need to be changed again but he hoped they would be in a safer place by then.

Taking a deep breath, the boy closed his eyes and let a light sleep set in.

7

The boy drifted on and off to sleep over the next few hours. As he tried fighting off sleep, he began dreaming of a large, lavish dinner party. He was dancing in a great hall with his sisters while his mother and father watched from their table. At one point from under a table, the boy stole a shoe from a well-dressed woman and held it up like a trophy, declaring the feat a small victory in his mind.

A sudden jolt caused the boy to lean forward and knock him out of his slumber. For a moment, the boy's eyes adjusted to his surroundings, before Luka opened the door to the closet, his face set with intensity.

"You must be quiet. There are guards on the train inspecting every car." Luka looked around to see if anyone had spotted his whereabouts. Taking the jacket that he bought for the boy, he slid it neatly over the boy's head to shroud him even more from possible sight.

The boy held the jacket in place as Luka closed the door, sealing him in darkness once again. He tried to maintain his breathing but was afraid that any indication might alert the guards. He practiced holding his breath but found the effort was much louder than breathing normally, so he attempted to maintain his normal breathing.

He heard the door to the private room slide open and a couple sets of heavy footsteps entered.

"We need to see your ticket please." One of the guards said, speaking to Luka. The boy didn't hear a response from Luka, but he had to have complied as the guard did not immediately question him again. "Headed to Nice, eh? Long trek ahead of ya." The guard's accent was much more intense than some of the others he had heard over the last few months. The guard was right though, Nice was quite a long distance from where they were leaving. The boy assumed they had at least another forty or so hours on the train. "You ain't seen any miscreant boys lounging around this car, have ya?" The guard seemed persistent.

"I've not done much looking, mostly sleep." Luka replied calmly.

Another voice sounded, this one much more stern than the first. "What is in Nice?"

"I have a nephew who is ill and needs proper care." Luka's voice remained monotone.

A few more moments of silence before the boy heard the first guard speak one final time. "You have a safe trip now. With the war on, some of these crossings won't be easy."

The boy heard the sliding of the door and then complete silence. A few minutes later, the train began to move again and the boy felt like he could finally breathe.

The closet door slid open slowly and the jacket was removed from the boy's head, revealing Luka staring at him. "Collect your things. We must move to the back of the train just in case we have another stop like this."

The boy did as he was told, grabbing his satchel and jacket from the closet. As Luka opened the sliding door, he peered out to see who was in the hallway of the train. It appeared empty as they stepped out and made their way down the hallway to the next car. He couldn't remember how many cars they had to go through to get to the back, but he was sure it couldn't be more than a couple.

As they passed through, the boy tried his best to hide his face from other riders, once again being forced to stare only at their feet and the red carpet beneath. He wondered if others tried to look at him as they walked by.

Once they reached the rear car, Luka opened the door as the boy looked up. The car was full of storage cases, most of which were unlabeled. He followed close behind as they made their way inside. Luka stood at the door as the boy made his way into the car, closing the door behind them.

"We'll be safe here for the rest of the voyage. Don't want anything like that to happen again. Who knows what they'll do if they catch you." He said as they moved further back towards the middle of the car behind a large storage container. "Now that they've checked the ticket, there shouldn't be any more stops like that." He placed his satchel on the ground near a crate and took a moment to stretch.

The boy became curious. "If you don't think the guards will be back, then why do we have to hide in the baggage car?" He felt as if Luka was hiding something, but he couldn't quite put his finger on it.

The old man looked at him briefly before turning back to sit down on the ground beside the crate. "You can never be too careful, boy. Eventually, someone is going to recognize you, if they haven't already. At least back here no one will bother us." The boy still wasn't sure if he could trust what Luka was saying. What had he seen that made him want to escape the private room? "That's also the most you've said since we've met." Luka let out a slight laugh. "Can't say I blame you. I wouldn't trust anyone either after..." He grew silent, realizing the weight of what he was about to say next.

The boy's curiosity seemed to run through him. "My family is dead; I do not wish to join them. What is our plan from here? I heard the guard mention our tickets were for Nice. France, I assume?"

"Indeed." Luka stretched again, sprawling his legs out in front of him. "The sooner we get you out of the motherland, the safer you'll be."

"What about the war?" The boy grabbed at his satchel, sitting down beside Luka. He had known the war had taken his father away from home for quite a while, and he knew that the battle seemed far from over when they were taken hostage.

"The war is heated, but nowhere near Nice, at least not now. Once we meet with my contact there, the goal will be to get you to Great Britain and reunite you with more family." Taking a small bit of bread from his bag, he proceeded to hand it to the boy. "How that will happen, I have no idea, but I'm sure Reggie can think of something."

The train ride lasted for a little over fifty hours, with a few stops in between. No other guards seemed to stop the train to do any further sweeps, but the boy was grateful that Luka had cared enough to hide them both from any danger. During the ride, the duo remained mostly silent, except for the occasional nods and Luka ensuring the boy was doing all right.

They ate most of what was inside their satchels during the ride, drinking bottles of water that Luka had stowed in his satchel. The pair slept in shifts, ensuring no one would enter the train car beside the two of them during the ride. Luka demanded that he be woken up at any point if someone else came in, but no one ever did.

At one point, the boy dozed off while Luka was on the lookout. Dreamland set in again and he was back with his family. This time, they were on a boat, but he had no idea where they were going. His oldest sister played some type of spinning game on the deck, spinning her dress left and right and in circles, seemingly making him feel dizzy. Looking over to his youngest sister, she appeared to be writing in her journal. This seemed strange to him since his oldest sister was the one who often journaled, not his youngest. He had written quite a few letters in his time but had failed to keep an accurate journal up to this point in his life.

He approached his sister, attempting to see what she had written down, but the pages appeared blank. Suddenly, his sister turned her head to look at him.

"This is your story." She said brightly to him. "It can be anything you want."

"What do you mean?" The boy asked, his sister turning her focus back to the empty journal.

Her face seemed to gloom over. "The path is treacherous, but the roads are plentiful. Great things can be accomplished. Or..." A drop of blood fell from her nose, spilling onto the journal and splattering on the page. The blood seemed to pool around one area of the off-white sheet, spreading out to reveal one word, 'Death'.

Blinking, the boy opened his eyes to find himself back in the train car. Luka was on the other side of a baggage hold, whittling another piece of wood. Straightening his back, the boy adjusted his position.

"You're awake." Luka responded, ceasing his whittling, and looking up at the boy.

"I am." The boy responded quickly, still thinking of the image from his dream, the picture of his sister spinning on the boat still stuck in his mind.

Luka took a deep breath as he stood up from his spot, stretching his arms out. "Good. We are almost twenty minutes from the station. I am going to do one final check before we depart."

The boy nodded in response as Luka passed by, pushing the train door open and then shut. He was then alone in the train car. Hearing the wheels and bearings spin outside made him long for silence again. A sense of peace that can only come from the quiet, something he felt he hadn't had in quite some time.

Gathering his satchel, he packed up anything that had fallen out and stuffed it back into the bag. On the ground was a piece of paper that covered the bread they ate. Grabbing it with one hand, he shoved it back into the bag. As his hand hit the bottom, he felt his fingers hit a sharp object, not sharp enough to cut but sharp enough to notice.

Withdrawing his hand, he peered inside to look at the object. It wasn't something he could see for how dark the train car was, so the boy slipped his hand back inside. Feeling the object, he clutched it in his hand and pulled it out. It appeared to be another piece of paper, wrapping something else. Carefully, he peeled away the paper to reveal a blue sapphire jewel, one that had been embroidered into his jacket. He figured that Klara had hidden the jewel in his bag before he left. The object seemed to send a slight grin to the boy's face before melting into sadness. He knew that she had good intentions of giving him the jewel, but it seemed to only remind him of what he used to have, and what was now gone.

Taking a deep breath, he placed the jewel back in the bag and closed the flap. A noise came from the front of the car as the boy looked above the baggage hold to see Luka returning from his check. He could feel the train begin to slow down, their destination only moments away. How long had he stared at the jewel?

"Got your bag?" Luka asked, walking over to grab his own from the other side. The boy once again nodded in affirmation. "Good. Let's get going."

The old man moved swiftly again towards the front of the car, the boy following close behind as instructed. As Luka opened the door to the next cabin, a huge beam of light burst through the car, illuminating the entire area. Stepping into the cabin, the boy noticed people were beginning to line up at the doors of the train.

As the train slowed even more, the appearance of a station came into view through the windows. He hadn't seen any of the view during the whole trip but the fact that he was seeing the train station made his heart full for some reason.

The jerk of the train as it came to a complete stop caused the boy to stumble, falling directly into Luka, who only grunted in response. Standing straight up, the boy watched as trainmen opened the doors one by one, releasing each car as they walked down the train.

Finally, the door to their car opened and everyone began to exit. As he stepped out, he began to feel more relaxed, and his senses seemed to fold into themselves. Looking around at his surroundings, the daylight shined brightly on his face as the tall stone of the station towered over him. The feeling of fear began leaving his brain, and he felt at ease.

As they walked by the trainmen, he could hear them greeting everyone with the same phrase. "Bienvenue à Nice." .

8

The surroundings in Nice were spectacular. As they journeyed through the station, the boy could see gorgeous buildings and small shops in a walkway just outside the main doors. The boy knew that Nice had a French military base but he never had the opportunity to travel there with his father during the military drills. The water from the sea was visible, about a kilometer away from where they were standing. The boy briefly hoped they would have time to see some of the sights during their stay, but that thought quickly faded when he remembered the reason he was there in the first place. He had escaped death in his own country, only to be accompanied by a stranger to a faraway land. Now the boy had other options to consider, and there didn't seem to be much time for sightseeing.

Once outside of the train station, the boy and Luka continued their journey to meet Luka's contact. Passing by the small shops and pâtisseries on their walk, the boy completely forgot about needing to keep his head down. Although, at this point he wondered if it was even necessary. Surely the guards would never suspect that he had fled to France.

Luka spoke about his contact on the walk through town. The man's name was Reginald Bellion III, but most people referred to him as Reggie. This man was a relative of Luka's, although the relation had never been made fully clear to the boy. The excitement in Luka's voice made the boy eager to meet him, but he was not sure of the reason for Luka's excitement. Still, the boy followed close behind for about fifteen minutes until they reached a tall stone building. The structure was massive with large windows and a red slated roof. Red shutters were bolted to the side of the windows so they would not move in the wind.

The front door of the structure was made of wood with a steel-framed window in the top center. The wood reminded him of the door he had walked through just a few nights ago with his family. The boy hung onto the phrase 'a few nights ago' in his head. Had it really been almost four days since he escaped? His mind raced in disbelief. So much had happened in a short span of time.

The door opened and what appeared to be a French guardsman stood in the doorway. His blue jacket bundled with a gold sash across his chest made him look like a very important person, although the boy wasn't sure if he was.

"Puis-je vous aider?" The guard asked with conviction in a low voice, but Luka did not respond. His silence caused the boy to look up at him. For a moment, the boy did not realize why Luka had not responded to the guard. Then it dawned on him; Luka did not speak French.

The boy stepped forward with one quick swoop to face the guard. "Nous aimerions aller voir M. Reginald Bellion III." He hoped that his French was correct, it had been months since he took a French lesson, and he often missed speaking to his French tutor. The guard paused for a moment before smirking and opening the door the rest of the way for them to enter.

"Please come in." The guard stated this time in English. The boy was taken aback by this statement before following Luka inside. The entrance of the building was massive. Stone walls adorned with portraits of army generals and swordsmen from days long past, with swords and guns decorated in between. The boy assumed this had to be some kind of military palace, used for housing members of the French infantrymen before going off to fight in battle. The place appeared to be a military aficionado's dream.

"Uncle Luka!" A voice shouted from the other end of the extensive hallway. A tall man with sandy blond hair a little darker than his approached them, wearing a similar jacket to the one the guard was wearing who let them inside. He looked to be about twenty years old. The boy also took note of the term the man said. 'Uncle', thinking that he might have misheard Luka telling him about this man earlier.

A smile appeared on Luka's face, wider than the boy had seen up to this point. "It's good to see you, Reggie." As the man drew closer, the two men met with a handshake in the middle, causing Reggie to smile almost as wide as Luka.

"Please, let's head upstairs. We can get you a bite to eat and some beds. There will be much time for conversation later." Reggie stated, getting a glimpse at the boy before quickly darting his eyes away. It was as if he was scared to look at him. The boy hung his head in response.

They proceeded up the stairs and into a room where two beds were made up. The room seemed too large for only the two beds, making him think they had been placed there shortly before their arrival. Along the wall was a gentleman's chest placed evenly between the two beds.

"Set your things down and relax. I will have Renée bring you something to eat." Before either of them could respond, Reggie was flagging down a girl in the hall. She peeked into the room as he spoke to her in French, requesting food for the two men. The young girl nodded and left. Reggie stepped back inside and closed the door. "It has been ages, Uncle Luka. Five years, almost?"

Luka sat down on the bed, attempting to make himself comfortable. "Aye. Five years next month. You've grown into such an incredible young man." He reached for his satchel and placed his hand inside.

"Not bad for twenty-three years, eh?" Reggie smirked again. The boy enjoyed seeing the two men together as if they were old friends. "You're still just as spry as ever! Taking a train for almost fifty hours to Nice!"

"Had to be done." Luka responded, his hand finally escaping his satchel. In it, a red jewel glistened from the light shining through the window. Another jewel from the boy's jacket, he was sure of it. "This is from Klara. A token of our appreciation, and a token of passage for..." Luka looked over at him this time, causing the boy's mouth to open slightly.

Grabbing the red jewel, Reggie held it up to the light. The boy could see there were imperfections in the jewel, justifying his suspicion from earlier. "So... this is the one that all of the fuss is about." Reggie continued looking at the boy, away from the jewel, never darting his eyes. He smiled. "This is the crown prince."

"He has a name, Reggie. And he should be treated with the same respect." Luka scolded Reggie as soon as the words left his mouth.

Reggie's smile faded a bit, leaving behind a sheepish grin. "Of course, Uncle Luka. Where are my manners?" He approached the boy and knelt in front of him, head bowed briefly before looking back up and returning his gaze. "It is a pleasure to meet you, Alexei Nikolaevich; Romanov heir to the Russian throne."

9

This was the first time in almost six months the boy had been called by his title. The last person to call him by that name was his father. His sisters and mother would only refer to him by his first name. Now, a French guard named Reggie was calling him the name no one would dare speak in Russia; 'Alexei Nikolaevich', or 'Alexei Romanov'. The latter part of the title is what sent chills down his spine. 'Heir to the Russian throne'. The Russians had been searching for him, and hearing his name out loud felt like it breathed his status into existence, like a smoke signal rising into the air.

By the time Alexei came out of his thoughts, Reggie looked over at Luka with a concerned face, shrugging as if not knowing what to do next. Luka looked back at him before responding. "You must be cautious with a young man who has recently lost his entire family, even if he is a prince." With that, Luka stood and knelt, mimicking Reggie's movements. "It is an honor to serve, Alexei Nikolaevich."

Two times now his name had been said in the last minute.

He feared that the guards might storm in and arrest him right then and there. He looked down at both Reggie and Luka, who were still kneeling at his feet. The boy's face began to turn red. He never liked when people bowed or kneeled before him as he was not sure how to properly respond. "Please stand." Alexei said as the two rose to their feet.

Reggie peered back at Alexei, his face seemingly anxious. "Young prince, you must tell me what happened. I must know every detail to be able to help you."

Alexei's eyes darted through the room, looking for anyone who might be listening. "It is a long story..."

"Do not pressure the prince." Luka commanded. "He will tell you in due time. For now, let's see if we can eat and rest. The train ride was mighty unpleasant." He looked back at Alexei, giving a slight grin in response.

Reggie straightened his back. "Yes, let's talk later."

A knock at the door revealed the young girl from earlier, holding a tray in her hands. "Merci, Renée." Reggie responded, grabbing the tray from her hands and sending her on her way, closing the door on the way out. He placed the tray on Luka's bed. "There should be enough food here for both of you. Please let me know if you require more." With that, he stood up and made his way to the door. "Take this evening to rest. We will talk business tomorrow." Closing the door behind him, Alexei heard a slight click of the latch, signaling that the door had been locked. Anxiety crept in again.

"Don't worry, young prince. It is for your...our protection." Luka assured him. He felt like he could trust this old man by this point. The man looked so disheveled that he wondered about his own clothes and appearance. He looked down at the white buttoned shirt he was wearing. A couple of dirt stains horizontally smeared across, making it look like he had brushed up against something. His green vest was also tarnished in a few places with dirt and grime.

"Do you imagine they will let us bathe?" Alexei asked. Luka sat back down on the bed, opening the lid of the tray to reveal two hearty bowls of beef ragout and a large baguette to go along with it. Taking his first bite, Alexei felt an instant rush of happiness wash over him. This had to be the first meal in a very long time that reminded him of home.

The two each ate all their respective dishes, and neither could fathom eating anything else. Setting their bowls back down on the tray, Luka placed the lid on top and placed the tray on the floor. Swinging his feet up towards the bed, he laid his head back on the pillow. "I believe if you knock, they might let you out to bathe." He took a deep breath. "I think I will just lay here for a bit. It was a long journey, after all."

Within seconds, he could hear snoring come from Luka's side of the room. It had to have been only mid-afternoon by this point, but he could understand why Luka would be so exhausted.

Standing up, Alexei made his way to the door. Raising his fist, he gently knocked three times in succession. For a moment, he heard no one on the other side. Suddenly, footsteps could be heard approaching.

"Oui?" It sounded like the young girl from earlier, Renée.

He tried to recall his French. "Je voudrais…prendre un bain…s'il vous plaît."

Another moment of silence fell across the room until he heard the click of the door latch release and the door begin opening. Renée stood on the other side of the door; her green dress illuminated from the sun. She had to be in her late teens or early twenties.

"Suis-moi." She said quickly as she began to walk down the hallway. Alexei followed, shutting the door behind him to drown out Luka's snores. The hall seemed even bigger than before. More portraits, guns, and swords hung along the wall. Doors spread out evenly in between decorations. Finally, Renée stopped at the door at the end of the hall and turned toward him. "Voilà." One word was all she said before walking off in the opposite direction. Alexei was very thankful he could understand what she was saying, mostly because she wasn't speaking in complete sentences.

Placing his hand on the door, he opened it to reveal a large washroom, complete with a bathtub, sink, mirror, toilet, and bidet. For a moment, he felt as if he were back at the palace in St. Petersburg. The room appeared reminiscent of one of the washrooms on the first floor, positioned almost to the letter. Closing the door, he noticed a latch on the inside and slid it over to prevent the door from being opened by someone else.

Walking over to the mirror, he caught a glimpse of his face. The black marks on his shirt weren't just on his clothing. His face looked like it hadn't been washed in ages. Taking one of the washcloths from the counter, he proceeded to dampen it in the sink and wipe his face, allowing the dirt and grime to rub off.

Unbuttoning his white shirt, he noticed the patch that Klara had put on his wound before they left had started to peel. Taking his hand and placing it on the end of the bandage, he carefully peeled it away to reveal the wound. It looked a little better than it had a couple of days ago, and he was grateful that it looked like it was healing well.

A few years ago, he had fallen off a boat and split his leg open terribly. The wound refused to close, and the blood seemed to pour from it endlessly. Doctors said that he had a type of bleeding disorder but he could never remember the name, and his mother called it a 'family curse'. It took almost a month for the wound to finally start to improve and almost a full two months before he found himself walking again.

After bathing, he felt a huge sense of relief, as if months of filth had been washed away. He looked at his wound again in the mirror before taking some more gauze he found in a drawer nearby and patched himself up again. He wondered how long the bruises would last.

He thought about putting his old clothes back on and how it would make him feel. But instead, he searched the washroom for a change of clothes. Inside an armoire, he found a much nicer buttoned shirt that he replaced with his old one, buttoning it up to ensure that it fit. He also found a pair of trousers that were much bluer than the ones he had on before. He kept the green vest and slipped it back on before exiting the room.

Back down the hall, Alexei made his way toward the room where he had left Luka snoring away. He could almost hear the old man from the other side of the hallway. That's when he also noticed something else; the entire hall was now silent and devoid of people. The eeriness of his surroundings caused him to walk faster back to the room.

Quickly opening and shutting the door, he breathed a sigh of relief before returning to the bed that had been made for him. Propping up his feet on the foot of the bed, he laid his head down on the pillow and stared up at the ceiling. He still wasn't sure he could trust Reggie yet, but he had to give him some credit as Luka was the one who thought of the idea to bring him here in the first place. He figured he would rest on it. The bed was much more comfortable than anything he had slept on in ages and he wondered if this would be the only night he would sleep in something this cozy.

Alexei shut his eyes and wandered off into dreamland again.

10

When Alexei finally opened his eyes, he could see the sunlight beaming through the window onto the blanket he was wrapped in. He wondered how long he had been asleep as he stretched his arms and allowed his body to pull itself straight. Throwing off the blanket, he tossed his feet toward the ground before feeling slight tension in his back. The last few days on the train had not been the most pleasant, and his body was paying the price.

Looking over to the other side of the room, Luka's bed was empty and made. He thought that he should do the same, so he turned and made his bed before throwing on his boots and proceeding to the door. Twisting the knob, it barely budged before a click sounded on the other side, opening to reveal a French guard outside waiting for him.

"Bonjour, petit garçon." He cringed at being called a little boy but attempted to shrug it off. "Les autres sont en bas." The guard stated, informing him the others were already downstairs waiting on him.

"Merci. Allons-y, s'il vous plaît." He gave the guard a slight nod to lead the way and they made their way down the flight of stairs to the main hallway. He took more notice of the portraits that were on the wall. His eyes could not believe the vast number of items that were hanging. Almost every inch of the walls were covered. Even the stairwell was adorned with epaulets from days of soldiers past.

Alexei was certain the rest of the house had no idea who he was, at least not at first. There were probably curiosities that wandered around of a young boy taking refuge in a military building, but he had to be sure that Reggie had not given him away that easily. The guard didn't seem to take notice of him at all, merely following orders to bring him downstairs to where they were meeting.

Taking a right at the bottom of the stairwell, they made their way towards another wooden door guarded by two more soldiers in uniform. The mere look of the scene sent chills up his spine for a moment before he could collect himself.

One of the soldiers turned and opened the wooden door, revealing another rather large room, resembling an office. On the right side of the room sat a desk adorned with books, papers, and quills. A sturdy bookshelf sat behind the desk, filled to the brim with books on each shelf. To the left sat a fireplace with three chairs. In one sat Reggie, seemingly dressed in the same uniform that he wore yesterday. In the other sat Luka, smiling, and talking away with Reggie as if he hadn't a care in the world.

He watched as the guard ushered him in, then immediately turned around and left, closing the door behind him. Everyone acted so suspicious, but he attempted to pay them no mind as he walked over toward the inactive fireplace.

"Ah, the young prince is awake." Reggie said with a grin. Luka shook his head again in disbelief.

"I thought I told you to refer to him as..."

Alexei interrupted Luka. "Please, you may refer to me as anything you wish." This comment seemed to stun the old man as he sat back in his chair.

Reggie kept his grin and motioned toward the empty chair. "Sit, young prince. We've much to discuss."

Alexei made his way over to the vacant chair and sat down. The plush red cushion was a delight to sit on, almost making him want to bounce up and down, but he refrained.

Grabbing his glass from the table beside his chair, Reggie began to speak again. "First of all, how are you fairing this morning? You slept the whole evening and night. We were worried you'd slipped into a coma."

Luka glared again at Reggie before scolding him. "That is not in the least bit funny." Although he could tell that the old man found at least some humor in it. The scolding seemed to be that of proper stance than of actual discipline.

"I am feeling better. Thank you for your concern." Alexei adjusted himself in the chair, attempting to make himself more comfortable. "Thank you for taking us in. Your generosity is greatly appreciated and will be repaid."

"It is an honor." Reggie said as he took a sip of his drink and placed it back down on the table. "We will ensure the safety of the royal family...er...whatever's left of it." The comment almost made him sick to his stomach, but Reggie went on. "Speaking of that, I believe you owe me a story. Uncle Luka has brought you all this way and it is my duty to safely get you where you need to go next, but I must know the circumstances that I might find myself in."

Alexei straightened his posture. "You are aware of my father's abdication?" His father Nicholas had given up the throne almost a year and a half ago, just after their capture.

Reggie hung his head slightly. "Yes, the world is aware of that." He went to grab his drink but removed his hand suddenly. "We know of your capture and your family's imprisonment. Up until now, we have been told that you all were safe. I'm assuming from what Luka has informed me, that is not entirely true."

"That would be correct." Alexei shifted again. "After our capture, my family was taken to Siberia. We remained there for quite some time, in a cramped house guarded by Russian soldiers every hour of the day, even as we slept. They moved us a few times, but I believe we remained in Siberia for much of our time in capture."

"That must have been boring for you as a twelve-year-old boy." Reggie said cautiously.

Alexei nodded. "It was, indeed. I was only allowed to play with a couple of children in the area, mostly from the soldiers' families." He took a deep breath. "We were in Siberia for over a year, until one night when my mother, father, and oldest sister were taken, leaving my three youngest sisters and myself." He hesitated before speaking again. "I...had injured myself pretty severely about a month before that, so I was not able to travel." He could tell both men were waiting for an explanation. "I sled down a flight of stairs and hit my thigh on the banister on the way down. The impact caused major bruising and the doctors were worried about hemorrhaging, so I was not allowed to leave because of...the family curse."

"A royal curse, or so I've heard." Reggie stated it as a fact. Alexei nodded in agreement. "From your mother's side, I presume. Queen Victoria's lineage."

"Yes, so when my mother, father, and Olga were taken to Yekaterinburg, Tatianna, Maria, and Anastasia remained with me, at least for the next few weeks. During that time, I started to feel much better and was able to walk again. I noticed that Maria and Tatianna were doing a lot more sewing than usual. I approached them one day to ask about this, seeing that they were sewing jewels into my jacket pockets. I questioned the comfort of such a thing, and they responded that the purpose was not for comfort, but for my protection. They did the same for my youngest sister, Anastasia."

Another deep breath, he tried to keep from breaking. "Eventually, we were all reunited in Yekaterinburg. My mother wouldn't let me out of her sight almost the whole time. She watched me like a hawk, trying to ensure that I wasn't going to tumble down any more stairs."

Reggie was jotting down notes when he chimed in. "So,

your family was in Yekaterinburg for quite some time then?"

"A couple of months at least. It's hard to keep track of time when every day feels the same." Alexei looked over at Luka, who knew what was coming next. "Everything remained the same until one night, all of us were woken up in pitch black and told to get dressed. We did as we were instructed and were then told to follow a pair of guards to our next destination. We thought we were being moved again, maybe even rescued. None of us were allowed to read a newspaper or speak anything about the war going on outside. We arrived at a seemingly abandoned house and were guided to a cellar. Anastasia clung onto me the whole time, ensuring that I didn't fall behind." A tear began to fall from his eye as he brushed it away. "Once in the cellar, they instructed us to the middle of the room where about four...maybe five chairs sat. My mother and sister were insistent that I sit in one, and so I did." Another tear formed at the bottom of his eyelid, but he didn't wipe it away this time. "The rest is very blurry. I believe a couple of guards came into the room and began reading something. My father stood up...and..."

"Enough." Luka said sternly. "Reggie, this boy has been through enough torture to have to relive it over again just for your insight." Reggie put his pen down and looked at Luka.

"It's okay, Luka." Alexei said calmly, realizing that was the first time he ever said the old man's name aloud. He took another deep breath before continuing. "I remember the gunshots, but they sounded like ringing in my ears. I remember falling to the ground, my side in excruciating pain. Then, I remember waking up and being surrounded by my family, none of them alive." He thought about his sisters' lifeless bodies, his father's wide-open stare, and his mother's somber appearance.

"That's when he escaped." Luka interrupted. Alexei nodded, allowing him to continue. "I saw the boy hop out of the truck and dash into the woods. I followed him only because he looked familiar. It wasn't until I caught up with him that I knew who he was."

Reggie seemed to be fascinated by the story. "And now

you're here, the crown prince, standing in front of me, in Nice of all places." He set his pen down. "This is quite a story. One day, the world will know this courageous journey...but not today." He stood up and walked over to Alexei, kneeling in front of him, but not to bow. "Your journey has been long but know that it has only just begun. We are but a haven in a minefield, young prince." He looked at Luka before continuing. "Regardless, you've come all this way, and I intend to see you safely to London."

Alexei looked up at him. "London?"

"Yes, you have family there, do you not? A family that must be willing to harbor you until it is safe for you to come out of hiding." Reggie stood up and began pacing as if attempting to think of a plan. "We just have to figure out how to get you there first."

The young boy hesitated again before responding. "Do you think that his royal majesty would do such a thing? Harbor a prisoner of an allied country?"

Reggie grasped at his hairless chin. "I am unsure." He paced a few more steps. "Still, Russia has not made it clear that the Tsar and his family have been murdered. In fact, it is quite the opposite."

Alexei paused before looking up at him. "What do you mean?"

Reggie sighed. "The Russian militia released a statement just yesterday that the Tsar and his family are alive and well." The news made Alexei's jaw drop in disbelief. How could they hide such a heinous crime? "Announcing anything different would cause dissension in our ranks, and we must remember which side of the war we fight on."

Attempting to put himself back together, Alexei shook his head and leaned back in his chair. "What do we do now?"

Turning back toward him, Reggie placed his hand upwards toward him. "We will keep you here until I know what we must do next. You will be safe inside these four walls. No one knows who you are. They think you are an orphan that I am training for our military, brought here by my uncle."

Closing his eyes, Alexei attempted to think of a better plan, but couldn't come up with anything. He opened his eyes and turned back to Reggie. "It will have to work. Thank you."

11

The remainder of the day seemed to fly by. After speaking with Reggie and Luka, Alexei remained in the office for a good portion of the day. He requested materials to read up on the ongoing war, the imprisonment of his family, as well as anything culturally beneficial that they felt he should know. He immersed himself in the newspapers and journals the staff provided him, most from the last few weeks.

The Great War had been raging on for almost four years now. Browsing through certain articles, it seemed as if the Allies were on the winning side, with the United States joining them in April of last year. Kaiser Wilhelm II of Germany seemed to be getting scared of the advances the Allies were making and looked to be scrambling to bolster his offensives. Alexei was pleased to hear these results, remembering that his homeland was on the winning side. He wondered if the cards would begin to fold in favor of the Allies sooner rather than later.

Before their capture, Alexei had journeyed with his father to visit many of the soldiers and battle grounds in show of support, as well as watch his father give uplifting speeches. He remembered his father remaining resilient during that time, watching as he would tower over his audience from the podium while he watched directly behind him. His father had always shown incredible courage. He only wished he could hear one of those speeches again.

Turning his attention to the newspapers regarding his family, he noticed a lot of photographs were being used to show the royal family still in good health. Of course, these photographs were much older than the newspapers were letting on. In fact, Alexei was just eleven in one of the photos a newspaper printed just last week. He read about their imprisonment, Russia stating that the royals were being kept imprisoned in St. Petersburg, and nothing about being moved to Siberia where they had been for almost a year. A lone photograph of his sisters was captioned 'the young princesses enjoying a stroll in a St. Petersburg Garden'. Sure, the garden may have been in St. Petersburg, but that photo was taken at least two years prior. It was as if the papers had frozen his family in time, but perhaps that was their sense of security without fearing for the worst.

Anger started to rush through him as he thought about what those guards had done that night to his family. The resistance had to be behind this. His father had served greatly to ensure the resistance wouldn't revolt against him, tasking Russian secret police, the Okhrana, with hunting them down, but it appears that the resistance had done so anyway. Alexei heard that his father, the Tsar, wasn't the greatest at commanding the military, but the support of his military leaders also failed him in his time of need. A few of them must have turned to the resistance in order to have as much intel as they did on his father at the time of their capture.

A knock at the door disturbed his thoughts as Reggie peeked his head in, his blonde hair falling in front of his face. "Excuse me..." he stated as Alexei motioned for him to come in. "I apologize for the inconvenience..."

Alexei looked at him. "No, please do come in." He stood from the desk where the newspapers were scattered. "You'll have to excuse the mess."

Reggie waved a hand as he moved closer. "It is an understandable mess, crown...err..." he hesitated, seemingly unsure of what to say next.

"Alexei...is just fine." He said, beginning to walk around the desk to meet him.

Reggie seemed taken aback. "I...are you sure that alone would be proper? That seems very improper." He seemed to be sweating in his jacket as he pulled on it slightly around his neck.

Alexei's back straightened. "It is more than okay. In fact, I insist it is the way you address me from now on."

Looking down at the floor for a moment, Reggie thought before responding. "As you wish, Alexei."

The sound of his name instead of a title made him grin. "Now..." turning his attention back to business. "What can I do for you?"

Again, Reggie hesitated before speaking. He seemed much more nervous than this morning. "There is some news...out of Russia."

Alexei's ear perked up. "I am listening."

Closing his eyes, Reggie hesitated again. "It is regarding your father, the Tsar Nicholas." Alexei didn't speak, just waited for him to finish. "They are claiming that he has been killed by the Bolsheviks."

"This would be a correct statement I suppose." Alexei responded. "They would have had to admit it at some point."

Reggie's face scrunched a moment, his hands slightly balled up beside him. "Yes...but...my friend, he is the only casualty that they have admitted to."

Alexei's face froze. "What are you saying?" He watched as Reggie's fingers began to fidget.

"In a statement from the Bolshevik Regime, Tsar Nicholas has been assassinated for his attempted war crimes. The remainder of the royal family has been moved to a safe location;

all others unharmed." Reggie took a deep breath before looking at Alexei, whose face had begun to look as if it were melting.

Turning his back to Reggie, he made his way towards the window in the study, looking out to see the street and people passing by. "So, they are to create a government based on fallacy and lies." He took a breath before turning back to Reggie.

"It seems that way, my friend." He could tell his face seemed sorrowful to have to deliver the news. "The Allies will believe this, but this could work in our favor. One of the royals is, indeed, still alive. We could use this information to get you safely to Great Britain."

"That will be very risky." Alexei breathed again, his hands now starting to shake. "If my whereabouts are announced, I become someone with a target on their back, a larger target I should say."

Reggie nodded. "This is most likely correct. If I could share my thoughts?" Alexei nodded in affirmation. "I feel that keeping your status and location an absolute secret is the best option for now, not only for you but for France as well. While you are here, we will prepare you to take leave for Great Britain and I have shored up someone worthy to accompany you."

Squinting his eyes, Alexei became confused. "May I ask why you may not be that person?"

Reggie hesitated again. "If I were to accompany you, the journey would look suspicious. A mere aspirant would rouse the wrong kind of eyes journeying to Great Britain in a time of war. No...you would need at least a captain to accompany you. Anyone higher than that can travel between the allied countries with no problem whatsoever."

Thinking about what Reggie had just said, Alexei hung his head for a moment. "How long do you think it will take to find someone to accompany me?"

"With my resources, only a few days. For now, you can lay low and continue to research the events going on outside of these four walls. I am sure that you still have much to learn." Shuffling his feet, he seemed uncomfortable.

Alexei paused, trying to imagine a scenario where things might work out in his favor. "As long as my safety is not in question, I am fine to remain here as long as need be."

Reggie took a deep breath. "I am very relieved to hear you say that prince...erm...Alexei." He shuffled nervously for a moment. "With the war seemingly coming to an end, there may be a time where the trains will stall or become overrun, so it is important to act as fast as possible." Straightening his back, he looked at Alexei. "I will search out someone for the task of your extradition. Please know that you are safe here for the time being, dear friend."

12

Alexei rummaged through more papers to try and find information on his family for the remainder of the day, but most remained silent on their whereabouts and focused on the war. There were some articles, primarily opinion pieces, that remained skeptical of how safe the Romanov family was, but no one speculated that all the royals had been disposed of.

Hours had passed before Alexei realized the sun began setting outside the office window. Reggie had come in a few times to check on him, but he was shooed away almost as quickly as he entered. Others brought food and more articles they had found throughout the day, to which he tried to be grateful but kept his head down whenever they were in the room, attempting to look preoccupied. Reggie informed him the other soldiers were not suspicious of his presence, just that he was a boy looking to enlist and was wanting to stay informed about the world in the meantime. He wished there had been a way to lock the door though as the intrusions felt almost purposeful. He had felt alone for quite a while but in this moment, he wanted to be alone. His thoughts kept spiraling as to what to do next.

The young officer had shown quite a bit of remorse for the situation, although part of him felt as if no one would ever believe who he truly was again, especially if the Bolsheviks had any say in the matter. Reggie's plan of getting him to Great Britain had to be his best option. Surely King George would listen to his pleas and help restore proper order.

Packing the newspapers and journals into a neat stack, he picked them all up and made his way for the door to the hall, grabbing the handle with his hand. The hallway seemed to be quieter than it had been in the morning when he entered, seeing only a face or two pass by, none of whom were Reggie.

The stairwell was empty as well. It was as if everyone had gone home for the evening. Still, Alexei carried the stack upstairs and to his room, attempting to be careful not to trip and injure himself in the process.

The door to his room was closed as he inched closer to grab for the handle, pushing down to release the latch. Upon opening, the two beds on either side of the room looked the same as they did when he left this morning. Even Luka's absence remained the same.

Entering the room and placing the journals and newspapers on the nightstand next to his bed, he walked back over to shut the door quietly. He figured he might be able to peruse through more of the papers this evening if there was time. The more information he could learn about the war before his journey, the better prepared he felt he would be.

A slight knock came from the door. "Your highness." Luka's voice said from the other side. Walking over, he opened the door to let him in.

"Alexei, please call me Alexei." He stated, attempting to lighten the situation.

Luka stared at him for a moment. "I will do no such thing!" He entered the room and began to make his way to the bed. Alexei shook his head at the old man's resistance. "Reggie might be able to get away with nicknames, but you are still the crown prince to me, and I will not dishonor you by saying differently."

Alexei grinned. "I do not take offense to nicknames. I prefer it." He looked at Luka's confused expression. "I've never been too keen on positions or titles."

Seeming to ignore his last comment, Luka continued. "What have you learned?"

He told Luka about the war and his family, also mentioning the announcement of his father's death. He found it odd that Luka's expression never changed. It was as if he was expecting the information, including the news about the Tsar.

Luka took a deep breath. "So, it seems that the war may be coming to an end soon. This is good news for all of us." He shifted on his bed before looking back at Alexei. "I've spoken to Reggie, and he has told me what he plans to do." Alexei looked up at him, not knowing what he was going to say next. "At first, I thought it might be too risky...but it is surely the only way forward and the safest way at that."

Suddenly, Alexei felt a sense of immense sorrow. He hung his head as he spoke. "What if it is not?" Luka stared at him with questioning eyes. "What if I were to change my name, erase my identity, and start over as someone else?"

"You don't think that the Bolsheviks will look for you?" Luka's eyes now gazing into his. "Even if you try to erase yourself, your identity is written all over your face. You are a Romanov, a grandchild of Queen Victoria, and the son of Tsar Nicholas II. You have the look of a descendant. They will not stop until they have found you, regardless of if you try to hide." He took another breath. "And what will happen when they do find you will depend on what you do next." This phrase caused Alexei to tear up. "If you hide, the crown prince, Alexei Romanov, will have died with his family in a basement in Yekaterinburg. If you fight, the world will know you have survived, and may even come to your aide to restore rightful order." A tear fell from Alexei's cheek as he wiped his eyes. "Russia has watched you grow up, your highness. The young man you have become was destined to do greater things than even your own father. Please do not think the world would abandon you so easily."

Another tear fell onto his trousers, causing him to look away in slight shame. He took a moment to compose himself before responding. "Thank you for your kind words, Luka. But I fear others might not be as welcoming as yourself."

Luka nodded. "You will never know until you try to press forward and survive. Give up now, and your decision has been made for you."

Alexei turned to face the window to see the last glimpse of the sun before it fully set. Every path felt like it led to more death, more destruction. He felt he had to trust those who he had come to know over the last few days.

Luka decided that he was finished with the conversation as he crawled into his bed, covering himself fully before taking a long breath and asking one final question.

"Who do you want to be, Alexei Romanov?" He drifted off to sleep as Alexei sat there, thinking about the question.

'Who do you want to be?'

13

The next morning, Alexei woke up to find that Luka's bed was empty, and his belongings were nowhere to be found. Quickly throwing the blanket off his body, he looked around for any sign the old man might still be around but found nothing.

Throwing on his boots, he opened the door to find a few more soldiers in the hall than previously. About six or seven of them marched down the hallway to their respective posts, occasionally eyeing each other. One of them noticed that Alexei had opened the door and quickly glared at him.

"Ah, the boy is awake." The soldier said in English. Alexei flinched at being called 'boy' but wasn't sure it was best to tell them about his real name at this time. He still wasn't sure who he could trust. "You've missed breakfast and guard duties. You're not even dressed for drills. How are you to perform like a soldier if you don't have the discipline to act like one?"

Alexei thought about what the soldier had said, remembering that Reggie had told everyone he was a boy who wanted to join the regime brought here by Luka. He looked at the soldier, who was standing in the doorway a few feet away from him. “You are right…sir…” he struggled to find a proper title, seeing that this soldier seemed only a few years older than himself.

The soldier rolled his eyes before responding. “You can call me Ivan.” The other soldiers seemed to maintain their pose, some slightly grinning at the soldier’s response. “It is a good thing that Officer Bellion vouches for you. Nobody else would allow such behavior in the training hall.”

He had forgotten for a moment who the soldier was referring to, suddenly remembering Reggie’s last name. “I deeply apologize…Ivan.” The soldier flinched as his name was said aloud. “I will do better.”

“Officer Bellion waits for you in the study. You should hurry to see him.” Ivan stated as his eyes looked forward as if forgetting he was even there.

“Merci.” Alexei said, though Ivan’s facial expression did not seem to recognize the words. Making his way towards the stairwell, he noticed a few of the guards were staring at him, before darting their eyes back to their upright forward stance.

Descending the stairs, he noticed more soldiers were walking around, their boots shuffling against the marble floor of the entryway as they passed by. None of them seemed to take notice of him as he reached the bottom step, instead choosing to ignore him and carry on with their duties, whatever they may be.

Alexei turned his attention toward the study and took a few steps forward, noticing already the door was cracked open slightly as if he was expected. He approached the door and knocked three times.

“Oui?” He heard Reggie’s voice on the other side. He opened the door to see the sandy blonde-haired man staring out the window before turning back to notice him. “Ah, do come in.” He did as he was instructed, shutting the door behind him. “I had expected you earlier.”

Alexei hung his head slightly, noticing his brownish hair

falling into his face. "Yes, I do apologize for sleeping in." He thought for a moment before lifting his head to respond. "Where has Luka gone?"

Reggie looked at Alexei with a hint of sorrow. "He left this morning." Alexei's eyes darted away quickly to avoid showcasing his annoyance and hurt. "Boarded the train back to Koptyaki first thing at sunrise." He couldn't believe the old man would just leave without any kind of notice. The thought of Luka leaving made him feel abandoned. Reggie's eyes fell low as well. "I understand that he might not have been the best at goodbyes. That is Uncle Luka for you."

Remembering what Luka had said, Alexei reflected on where he had come from. The last few days had been a whirlwind of fight and survive. Now, he felt as if he were playing catchup with the rest of the world while still trying to figure out his next move. What he did next would determine the type of man he was, and the type of leader he would become if he were given the chance.

"I do have other news." Reggie stated, attempting to draw attention from the sadness that filled the room. Alexei looked up and nodded. "I believe I have found someone who can help us in our pilgrimage." This caused his ears to perk up.

"You have?"

"Yes. A general in the army who I am very well acquainted with has heard the rumors and reached out to me. I have not informed him that I know one way or the other of the royal family's sudden demise, but I have invited him here this evening for dinner and drinks. If all goes well, I should be able to secure whether he is trustworthy enough to see you to Great Britain, and perhaps arrange an introduction as well." Alexei's face seemed stunned. "That is, if you are up for entertaining such a thing."

He shook his head, feeling as if in a trance. "Yes, of course." Thoughts began spiraling in his head. "Things are moving much faster than I had anticipated."

Reggie approached him and placed a hand on his

shoulder. "Just remember, this is only the start. If we can procure the General, then we'll move into making the necessary arrangements to see you to Great Britain. That part of the plan may take another few days, I would think."

Alexei's anxiety seemed to calm with that statement. "Yes. That will allow me time to finish the newspapers and journals as I am sure I will not be able to take them with me."

"Maybe a few." Reggie smiled at Alexei, causing him to grin in return.

"Can you tell me about this general?" His curiosity seemed to spike in an instant.

"Of course!" Reggie said in an almost elated tone. "His name is LeBlanc, General Hugo LeBlanc. We met about a year ago on our deployment to Austria. His forces were some of the ones that helped to push back the regime, giving us a slight advantage. With the aid of the Russian forces, we were able to move the lines in our favor. He's a brilliant man, and I do think that you will like him."

Pausing for a moment, Alexei attempted to take in the information. "Do you truly feel that we can trust him?"

Reggie smirked. "He has never made an ill comment toward the Russian royalty, or any royalty for that matter. I've even heard he's been courting a great-granddaughter of the late Queen Victoria."

The last comment made Alexei roll his eyes slightly. It seemed as if Reggie was attempting to win General LeBlanc his favor without even being introduced. "Let us hope that he is as gracious of a man as you say." He turned as Reggie grinned again. "Will there be anything else? I would like to eat breakfast and continue my studies."

Heading towards the door, he heard Reggie cough to gain his attention. "I do have one more thing for you, Alexei." He could tell that he was still trying to get comfortable saying his name out loud. Reaching into his pocket, he pulled out a rectangular piece of paper that had been folded up. "Luka left this for you."

Immediately, Alexei's body turned around and he walked towards Reggie, almost snatching the piece of paper from his hands. Unfolding it, he wondered what Luka might have said to him before he left. He felt a slight sense of relief that he had not left without saying goodbye. The letter was short.

'Your Illustrious Highness,

Please do not think it rude of me for leaving you at this time, for I know you are in capable hands. I must return to Koptyaki to see to matters there. Klara and Shep are expecting me, and the farm work does not complete itself. Do not forget what I said. You are a bold young man with a future that you get to decide on. Remember who you are and determine who you want to be. Perhaps, one day, you will return to Russia, and we will be able to see each other again. Until that time, your journey to reclaim your right starts today. Do not dwell in the past but look forward to what is to come. I've left you a gift in your satchel, please do with it as you wish. Perhaps it will come of use on your journey. I pray that our paths cross in happier days.

Luka'

For a moment, Alexei felt happiness wash over him. He hadn't received a letter since his imprisonment where he had communicated with his tutor. Folding the letter back into a rectangle, he slipped it into his vest pocket before looking at Reggie, who had turned back around to face the window.

With that, he showed himself out of the study and made his way back upstairs, noticing the soldiers were much fewer in number than when he came down. At the top, Ivan still maintained his post, this time at his bedroom door.

"Finished already?" Ivan spoke, seeming skeptical.

Alexei grinned. "He gave me the day off." Opening the door, he noticed Ivan's facial expression change to irritation as his face faded from view.

His satchel lay at the foot of his bed. Walking over, he

picked it up and sat down on the bed before rummaging through it. Inside were some extra clothes that Luka had left for him, as well as a small sack. Reaching for the sack, he heard the clang of multiple items hitting each other.

The sack was made of thin rope, and Alexei could have sworn he had seen it before. Loosening the strings at the top, he peered inside to see a variety of colors staring back at him. Placing his hand below, he poured a couple of them into his hand. Out poured a variety of jewels; the ones that had been sewn into his jacket. Some of the jewels had traces of blood still on them, though most had been cleaned thoroughly. The jewels instantly reminded him of his sisters and how they had cared so much to protect him from harm. *'Perhaps it will come of use on your journey'.*

He placed the jewels back into the bag as tears formed in his eyes. "Thank you, Luka."

14

Alexei spent most of the day in his room, rummaging through more and more documents to gather information on recent events. He had been imprisoned for so long that everything seemed so foreign to him. He had forgotten life outside the four walls carried on even though he was kept away from it.

Reading through a few of the newspapers, he noted a slew of interesting facts. One of the first things that caught his eye was that women in Canada were granted the right to vote in May of that same year. Alexei had always thought women should have a stronger say in government, especially after hearing his eldest three sisters discuss politics. They seemed to be better versed in political issues than some men, sometimes including his father. This issue was always a point of contention in his household. His father disagreed with women having the right to vote, despite having four strongly opinionated daughters. Hopefully, other countries would soon follow Canada, perhaps even his homeland.

Another interesting fact that he noticed was the emergence of something called the 'great flu'. It appeared to be a deadly virus that began sweeping through the United States in March and has since been seen in Europe over the last couple of months. The mortality rates seemed to be isolated to children and the elderly, but the cases reported in each subsequent newspaper seemed to ebb and flow. He thought about himself for a moment, wondering if his inheritance of the 'royal curse' would make him more susceptible to such a virus. He attempted to shake off the feeling, thinking about the wound in his ribs. He had survived a murder attempt. He wasn't going to let the royal curse, or this illness bring him down.

Another interesting event he noticed was the attack and sinking of the RMS Carpathia. The Carpathia had been responsible for rescuing survivors of the RMS Titanic. Now, it lay at the bottom of the ocean, much like its sister ship. He was only six years old when the Titanic sank, but it was still ingrained in his brain to this day. Both his father and mother had friends on board at the time, most of whom did not survive. Now, the Carpathia has suffered the same fate, albeit with most passengers saved.

Observing the date of the sinking, Alexei noticed it happened on July 17th, the same day his family was awoken in the middle of the night, taken to the basement, and shot mercilessly. Chills ran down his spine as the thought crept into his mind. Sorrow had come and gone, and he felt that the time to mourn his family had passed him by many times over. The time for action crept closer.

He thought for a moment about his cousin, King George V, an almost spitting replica of his father. The last time he had seen the man was three years ago, just before the attacks became too heavy to travel the country safely. It was always strange to see Cousin George and his father together. It was as if they were twins separated at birth. The image of both men standing next to each other seemed unreal. Alexei sometimes had difficulty differentiating the two when he was younger, once asking Cousin George for a ride on his shoulders, mistaking him for his father. Cousin George had laughed it off and motioned him towards Nicholas. A year later, Cousin George had been crowned King of the United Kingdom. Although his father had meetings with him afterward, the remainder of the family was never allowed to travel due to the war, and they never saw him after that.

Attempting to shuffle through more newspapers, he found other articles pertaining to the war. In March, Moscow had been deemed the capital of Soviet Russia, marking a turning point in the Russian leadership after his father's abdication. March also seemed deadly for Great Britain, as almost twenty thousand army men had died from something known as the 'Spring Offensive'. In June, Italy managed to sink an Austrian battleship, and America's entrance into the war seemed to mark a turning point for the Allies. Great Britain had also formed an anti-Bolshevik army to interfere with the dual rule occurring in Russia, but Alexei felt this seemed like an afterthought.

So many more articles and newspapers awaited Alexei as he looked at the clock. Almost four hours had passed, and he had completely forgotten to eat. He took a pause and ventured downstairs to the small dining hall, where he found some fresh fruit, bread, and soup. He sat in the hall along with some of the other soldiers, watching as they glanced over at him and quickly looked back at their plates. He didn't seem to mind much though. They hadn't a clue who he was; just some vagrant training to fight alongside them.

A man's figure appeared beside him in uniform. Looking up, he could clearly make out the face of Ivan as he sat down next to him.

"You don't mind, do you?" Ivan stated, making himself comfortable before taking a bite of his food.

"Of course not." Alexei picked up his bread and began to dip it in his soup. For a few moments, there was nothing but silence as Ivan picked up his bread and began to eat it. He decided to do the same. Small talk was not something that came easily to Alexei. Instead, he concentrated on the food in front of him.

A few minutes passed until Ivan finally broke the silence, his mouth still half full of bread. "So, what brings you all of the way to Nice?"

Alexei hesitated a moment, swallowing his bread before responding. "I would like to train and fight, just like you."

Ivan squinted his eyes. "Is that so?" He took another bite of his bread. "Why aren't you fighting with the Russian army then?" A sudden chill ran down his spine. "You are Russian, aren't you? It would seem more appropriate to fight in your own country."

Beads of sweat began to form on his forehead. What he said next could completely give him away if he was not careful. "I am a vagrant..." his brow became cold. "My accent is Russian, but my will is free. I will fight alongside whoever will teach me... so long as they are allies."

A furrowed brow and a grunt were all that Ivan responded with, which seemed to satisfy him enough for the time being. A few more moments passed before Ivan spoke again. "Un allié est un allié, n'est-ce pas."

Alexei looked at him, he could tell from the tone of his voice that Ivan still did not trust him. "Vous allez voir, Ivan". The comment seemed to startle Ivan slightly, making Alexei think that he didn't know that he spoke French.

"Lexi!" A voice shouted from the other side of the room. He turned his attention to see Reggie standing at the door, waving for him to follow. Standing up, he went to grab his leftover food when Ivan motioned for him to stop.

"You can leave it. I'm still quite hungry." He grabbed at the remaining bread and soup, dragging it over to the area where his food sat. Alexei nodded in confirmation and proceeded to make his way over to Reggie, who was beginning to tap his foot impatiently.

He hadn't been called 'Lexi' in a while. The last person to call him by that name was his sister, Anastasia. She had taken a liking to calling him Lexi over the last few years, and he became accustomed to it. For a moment, hearing that name made him wish he could see her again.

Eyes focusing back onto Reggie, Alexei could tell he seemed antsy. "Faster." His pace quickened slightly as he made his way towards the door as Reggie spoke again. "The General is not going to wait all day for you."

Reaching within a couple of feet of Reggie, he stopped. "The General? He's here?" His face flushed.

"Of course, he is! I told you that I would be meeting with him this evening. Come on, he's waiting for us." Reggie motioned again towards the door, and Alexei followed through the archway into the main hall, glancing back for a moment to see Ivan staring directly at him with a look of confusion and disdain on his face.

Ivan seemed to be quite an interesting character, seemingly wanting to know more about him but at the same time not liking any of his responses. Alexei tried to shrug it off as they approached a door to a room that he had not yet been inside.

The door slid open to reveal another large room, much larger than the study he had occupied earlier in the day. A row of statues lined the far wall, and a fireplace with three large chairs sat at the very end. Seated in the far-right end was a man in a dark blue uniform, adorned with medals on his lapel and bright yellow epaulets on either shoulder. In his hand, a large cap with a feathered plume stuck out of the front. By the look of his facial structure, the man appeared to be in his mid-thirties. His dark brown hair revealed flecks of gray, as did his beard. Noticing that we had arrived, he stood from his chair.

Reggie approached first with Alexei following close behind. "Hugo, this is the boy I was telling you about." He lifted his face towards the General, who squinted in return.

"This is him?" For a moment, the General looked surprised. "You mean to tell me that this scrawny young boy is indeed the crown prince?" His eyes fixated on Alexei's face. "You must know that I have a very hard time believing this."

In retrospect, Alexei couldn't blame the General for being skeptical. No one had seen him or his family for at least six months. How was anyone to know how much weight they had lost, or how marginally kept their grooming was? His hair had grown considerably, and a haircut was always out of the question. His sisters had trimmed their hair with scissors, but he would not let them touch his.

Reggie interjected. "Uncle Luka would not lie to me, nor I to you, General."

The General squinted harder. "Does he speak?"

"I do." Alexei said quickly, almost too quickly for the General's liking. "I apologize, words have not come easily these last few days." He hung his head slightly.

"I see..." The General began to circle the boy like a vulture hunting for prey. "Do you mind if I ask you a few questions then?" He nodded in response. "Who are your sisters?"

Quickly, Alexei responded. "Tatiana, Maria, Olga, and Anastasia." He continued. "Alexandra is my mother; Nicholas is my father."

"I did not ask who your mother and father were." His voice grew cold as he resumed his circling. "Tell me about the last few months."

He recounted his story to the General, just as he did to Reggie, relaying all the details of the stay in Siberia and the move to Yekaterinburg, followed by the final night there. Afterward, the General only seemed more agitated.

"The Russian forces have only told us of the royal family being held in St. Petersburg. These other journeys seem suspect to me." He thought for a moment, staring at Alexei's face. "But your resemblance is striking to the crown prince. If it is true that Nicholas is dead, as well as the rest of the Romanovs, this could stir trouble for the Bolshevik uprising if the Allies were to uncover this." His face turned away. "Do you know if you are being actively hunted?"

The phrase made him flinch. "I believe so." The General's

back faced him. "When we were on the train, a group of guards asked Luka about a boy traveling on the train. That is when Luka moved us to the baggage car for the remainder of the trip."

"I see." His stiffened posture gave him a hint that he still wasn't convinced.

Alexei reached into his inner vest pocket. "During our stay in Yekaterinburg, my sisters had sewn jewels from our family collection into my jacket for protection." He pulled out the satchel that Luka had given him, pouring the contents onto the end table next to one of the chairs. "These are the jewels that were used. Klara, Luka's wife, had taken the time to remove quite a few of them for me to do with as I see fit. Proving my lineage to you seems an appropriate task for this."

The General looked at the jewels intensely, noticing the scrapes and blood traces that remained on a few of them. "No vagrant could have jewels such as these." Turning to face Alexei, he kneeled in front of him, his face bowed to the ground. "You are who you say you are. I will do what I can to serve you, your highness."

Again, he became uncomfortable with the formality, shifting to his side before responding. "Please stand. There is no need for you to kneel to me."

Regaining his balance, the General stood stiff once again. "You are still a prince, no matter your father's abdication. I will see you to London safely as Reginald has requested of me."

A smile brimmed across Alexei's face. For a moment, all the fears he had felt over the last few days had washed away. Reggie was standing nearby, smiling just the same before leaping into the conversation. "I am very glad we could settle this matter. Now, who would like a drink?"

Reggie moved over to a table that sat between two Greek statues and began to pour a couple of drinks. The General continued staring at Alexei for a few more seconds before speaking. "I have not properly introduced myself, your highness. My name is Hugo LeBlanc, High General for the French Army. I serve the royal family and my country, and all pieces that should fall in between."

Alexei extended a hand, which seemed to throw the General off. He hesitated before taking it on his own. "You may call me Alexei." He peered over at Reggie. "Or Lexi, if you prefer." Reggie looked back and grinned.

"Alexei will do." General LeBlanc smirked.

15

"So, first things first, we will need to get you on a train in the middle of the night." General LeBlanc said as he took a sip of bourbon before continuing. "Then, once we're on the train, we can see to it that someone will meet you in London. The train ride is around six hours to Paris but once we're on, there should not be any issues."

Alexei avidly taking notes with a pen and paper as the General spoke.

"When we connect in Paris and hop the train and ferry to Great Britain, I'll take that opportunity to make sure our contact is ready. We'll have around ten hours, which should put us in London sometime in the morning. There is a Sergeant in the British military who I know. I will attempt to contact him as soon as I leave here this evening. Once I have shored up his involvement, of which I will need to tell him everything I know, I will book the tickets and return for you."

Reggie sat in the seat across from Alexei, watching as General LeBlanc laid out the plan in detail, seemingly taking it all in as he sipped on his bourbon.

Setting the pen on his lap, Alexei looked up. "Are we sure that we can trust this Sergeant?" LeBlanc looked at him sternly. "Forgive me, I just want to be sure we are not setting ourselves up for trouble."

"Sergeant Blackwell has been a dear friend of mine for quite some time." He sipped his bourbon again. "I do not think we will have any problem trusting him. He has been loyal to the royal family for many years."

"Very well." Alexei picked his pen back up. "I do have one other question." LeBlanc nodded, giving him the right to ask. "What is the ultimate plan once we arrive in London? Will we be meeting with King George? I would hope to have an audience with him."

LeBlanc sighed. "Once in London, you will be much safer. I will consult with Sergeant Blackwell to see what the necessary steps should be. As for an audience with King George, that I cannot guarantee." Alexei hung his head at his response.

Reggie interjected. "Surely the king would see him. He is family after all. I mean..." He stopped suddenly as if he had realized something.

Pressing his tongue in front of his teeth, LeBlanc glared at Reggie for a moment. "Are you both unaware of King George's position on the matter?"

Confused, Alexei looked over at him. "Position on what matter, exactly?"

Shaking his head, Reggie stood up. "Lexi hasn't been allowed to see the news, but what I believe you're referring to is only speculation."

Alexei stood, slightly stamping his foot on the ground in a childish manner. "I demand to know what Reggie is speaking about."

Taking a deep breath, LeBlanc ushered Alexei to sit back down, which he did. "About six months or so ago, there was a rumor that your father, Tsar Nicholas, sent a plea for extradition to the United Kingdom. Some say that the king denied the request, and others say that he ignored it completely. There is also speculation that he never received it. No one really knows the correct answer."

For a moment, time seemed to stop. Almost a year and a half had passed, and Alexei had been held captive. Now, he was learning that his cousin had the opportunity to save his family but didn't. His blood boiled in anger, clenching his fists as he thought about the situation. "You mean to tell me that all of this could have been avoided had we been granted asylum?" His face began to turn beet red.

Reggie and LeBlanc could see the frustration on his face, and both hesitated with a response. Finally, LeBlanc looked at the boy. "There is a chance that the king never received the letter. In fact, the whole thing could have been a rouse to make people suspicious of what might have been going on in Russia. Only King George knows that answer. I pray that one day you get the opportunity to ask him yourself."

Feeling his face flush, Alexei closed his eyes to collect his thoughts before responding. "Have the Sergeant make the request. I will speak with the king myself upon our arrival in London." Standing up, he could still feel himself beginning to calm down from his anger. "Now, if you'll excuse me, I feel as if I need a rest. General LeBlanc, I look forward to your news of our departure."

With that, Alexei exited the room and made his way back upstairs to his bedroom. Quickly climbing the stairs and walking down the hall, he opened the door and shut it just as quickly.

Without warning, tears began to stream down his face as he paced back and forth. His anger had been built up inside of him for only a few minutes, but it seemed to be more than he could handle. Thoughts raced around his cousin not taking the opportunity to save his family, and he wondered if the rumors were true. One thing was for sure, he needed to speak to the king himself. The answer could only come from him, anything else was mere speculation.

Sitting down on the bed, he attempted to calm down. He

felt a twinge of pain spring from his rib where his wound was still healing. Walking over to the mirror on the side table, he unbuttoned his shirt to check on it. The bandage he reapplied a day or so ago finally looked like it needed a change. He walked over to his bag and took out some bandage and began to peel away. The wound had healed a little more over the last day, but it still looked as if it might start bleeding at any time. Placing a new bandage on, he sealed it tightly with some extra tape he found in the washroom yesterday.

Finishing up, he buttoned his shirt and proceeded towards the bed. Slipping off his boots, he stretched out to make himself comfortable, once again feeling the twinge in his ribs.

Outside, the sun had just started to set. He wondered how many times he would see the sunset before he would leave this place. These thoughts crowded his mind as he drifted off to sleep.

16

The next morning, Alexei opened his eyes to a glint of sunlight peering in from the window. He had managed to sleep through the whole night without any nightmares or disturbances. Knowing that the next phase of freedom was close at hand, he couldn't help but smile faintly as he rose out of bed and planted his feet on the floor.

As he stood on the hardwood, he noticed his face in the mirror. The thirteen, soon to be fourteen, year old boy looking back at him had begun to regain some of his youthful glow. A few days out of danger had done wonders for him. His smile grew a little larger until he remembered he was alone, then his smile quickly faded. He wished that Anastasia could be there to see him.

Memories of his family raced through his brain again. Remembering the last time he had a conversation with Olga, his oldest sister, she had told him that she feared the worst was still yet to come. He had tried his hardest to assuage her fears, assuring her that good things had to come due to all the pain they had endured. She told him of their father and mother's struggle to maintain a conversation without an argument. Alexei felt that the close quarters and constant contact would have been the reason for this, but Olga assured him otherwise. She had heard them arguing over their safety. His mother had always been protective of him, and she felt that he should have been taken to the hospital when he had his accident. His father, on the other hand, disagreed, saying that having him out of their sight wasn't the best idea. In the end, it didn't matter, as Olga was told by the guards that, even if anyone did need to go to the hospital, they were not allowed outside the house. At the end of the conversation, Olga kissed his forehead and said goodnight before escorting herself off to bed.

A knock on the door startled him and he shook his head quickly to return to the present.

"Entrez vous." Alexei said in an almost demanding voice.

The door opened and Reggie peeked his head in. "Oh good, you're awake." He said as he entered the room and shut the door, dressed in a freshly pressed officer's uniform. "How are you this morning? It's awful early for you. From what I've seen, you're more of a 'brunch' kind of guy."

Alexei laughed at his joke. "I do apologize. My body must get used to change, in more ways than one."

"Understandable." Reggie walked over towards the window, also noticing that the sun was just beginning to climb over the houses on the other side of the mountains in the distance. "LeBlanc and I are going to ensure you have safe travels to the United Kingdom. He is scouting today to find your escort once you arrive."

"Does he know when the plan will be executed?" Alexei asked with slight hesitation.

Reggie looked back at him for a moment. "Not yet. I'm sure once he secures the contact, this Blackwood...well...Blackwell fellow, things will move quite quickly." He turned around to look at him. "The question is, what are we going to do until then?" He crossed his arms and tapped his foot, awaiting Alexei's reply.

For a few seconds, Alexei looked puzzled, staring at Reggie as if he'd gone crazy. Then, he had an idea. "Do you think it would be possible for me to train with you?"

Seemingly taken aback, Reggie responded. "You want to train with the soldiers?"

Alexei nodded. "I think it would be a good idea, don't you? Perhaps I could pick up some skills."

Reggie smirked. "It is a great idea. Let me get you a uniform and then we'll be on our way." Making his way over to the door, he opened it and yelled out. "Renée! Can you bring a fresh uniform, please? Soldier, not officer." Turning back to Alexei, he was still grinning. "Renée will bring you what you need. Get changed and meet downstairs for company breakfast. Then we will head outside for drills." With that, he walked out and shut the door behind him.

It wasn't but another few minutes until Renée knocked on the door, presenting a freshly pressed soldier's uniform. The greyish-blue coat and pants with brown boots were much better looking than what he brought with him from Russia. He took a couple of minutes to change clothing, allowing his white button-down to stay on underneath to keep the fabric from rubbing against his wound.

Attempting to slip on the boots, he found a leather belt and sash inside. Taking them out, he finished putting on the boots, ensuring that the pant legs were tucked neatly into them. Next, he threw the sash over his shoulder and wrapped the belt around his waist, attaching it in front to secure it.

Looking back in the mirror, he almost looked like a different person. He had worn the Russian military uniform in the past, but this uniform was more comfortable, most likely due to the warmer climate. Again, he thought about how much older he looked, taking another minute to gaze at his face. The uniform had added another level of sophistication that he hadn't seen in a long time.

Taking one final look, he nodded to himself and proceeded out of the bedroom door into the hallway. He noticed there were a few soldiers upstairs still getting themselves together as he moved down the hall toward the stairs. Some of the soldiers he spotted were ones he had noticed from the previous day, but there were a few faces he hadn't seen yet.

Descending the stairs, he could already hear commotion in the mess hall where the soldiers were eating breakfast. He hurried into the hall where he could see a good majority of them seated, most of them almost finished. Spotting Reggie on the other side of the room, he noticed there were a few open seats next to him. Rushing over to the serving trays, he grabbed a few items, an apple, some toast, a spoonful of jam, and a hard-boiled egg, and proceeded to make his way over to the table, sitting next to Reggie who gave him a slight nod of approval.

Sitting down, he noticed three other soldiers eating with Reggie who were adorned in officer uniforms, and he immediately felt out of place. He thought about moving but felt that it would make things even more awkward than they already were.

"Typically, we don't allow the soldiers to eat with the officers." One of the officers from across the table stated loudly. "But when you're friends with Reggie's Uncle Luka, I suppose we can make an exception for today." The man smirked at Alexei as he put his hand out to shake his. "Officer Jean-Pierre Dupont, nice to meet you."

"Lexi. Pleased to make your acquaintance." He wondered if it was odd that he didn't cite a surname. He noticed that Reggie had stuffed his mouth with food.

The other officer, who looked much older than the other two, glared at him before also stretching out a handshake. "Officer Marcel Beauford." Alexei nodded with the handshake but did not repeat himself.

Still chewing, Reggie interjected. "Day one drills are going to be spent with Officer Dupont. He'll be showing you basic moving techniques as well as formation techniques. All the soldiers who are in their first few weeks will be with you."

Officer Beauford, still stern-faced, spoke next. "I will take the ready recruits north today. We will bound a train for Paris to fly out as soon as possible to assist. There's still a war on, after all." From the sound of his voice, Officer Beauford did not seem pleased with the other two officers who were sitting next to him.

Reggie looked at Alexei. "I guess that leaves me to supervise the middle recruits with arms training."

Suddenly, something dawned on him. "Does everyone speak English here?" This caused Reggie and Officer Dupont to laugh as they looked at each other. Officer Beauford continued to eat, paying no attention to the question.

Officer Dupont picked up his glass of juice. "Reggie informed us that your French is...lacking. And, since none of us speak Russian, we thought that English was a better way to go." He took a drink and set the juice back down. "Be mindful though, a lot of the recruits do not speak English, so they will only speak French to you."

"Je sais assez." Alexei said as he bit into his toast. Dupont and Reggie grinned again.

After breakfast was over, the men split into three groups. Altogether, there seemed to be about thirty men, which surprised him as he didn't feel there were thirty bedrooms in the house, leading him to believe that most of these men shared rooms. Over half of the soldiers were taken by Officer Beauford to the train station departing for Paris to join the larger army, leaving only twelve of them behind. Five of the soldiers were escorted by Reggie to the shooting range and the other seven remained with Officer Dupont. Alexei looked at the remaining group and noticed another familiar face. Ivan, who had interrogated him yesterday and guarded his door, was also in his group.

Officer Dupont began to speak. "Recrues. Aujourd'hui, nous allons effectuer des exercices manœuvres. Sortez et attendez en ligne." The last sentence took Alexei a moment to translate in his head, but he followed the others outside. As he saw them lining up he followed suit and stood next to another soldier, one he had not interacted with until this point.

Strangely, everyone looked the same in their uniforms, the only things distinguishing them were their facial features and hair color.

Ivan stood on the opposite end of Alexei, seemingly ignoring his existence. He grew curious as to why that might be but tried to brush it off as Officer Dupont began to walk down the row, critiquing each of them in one way or another.

Upon reaching him, Alexei squinted slightly as Dupont looked him up and down. " Très bien avec l'uniforme, Monsieur Alexei." He breathed a sigh of relief.

The first activity had them marching in a straight line, narrowing down the ability to use their peripheral vision to detect people next to them, as well as to keep their footing. At the front of the field, a boy much younger than the rest, played a small drum to keep time. This went on for about an hour before Officer Dupont was satisfied with their progress, dismissing the young drummer boy back inside.

The second activity was formation and technique drills. Dupont took turns assigning a leader, and wherever the leader went, the rest of the chain had to follow, lining up in whatever formation was appropriate for the area. Each soldier took turns leading the charge for technique, moving around the yard, and allowing the others to follow and form around them when they stopped. When it came time for Alexei to lead, he moved forward towards the middle of the yard, then immediately shifted backward, causing the rest of the group to realign their stances as they marched beside him. Suddenly, he took off in a sprint, and the others followed his lead. He couldn't believe how much fun he was having. Stopping, the others formed two lines behind him.

"Très bien!" Officer Dupont called from the other side of the yard. "Suivant, Ivan!" With that, Ivan stepped in front of him, almost pushing him out of the way to take the lead. He sprinted off in the other direction, and the others followed. Alexei followed closely behind, allowing some space between the group and himself. Suddenly, the group was closing in on him. Ivan had turned around abruptly and was charging back into the group. As Ivan passed him, he felt a shove on his side where his wound was located, causing him to fall to the ground.

"Gringalet ..." He heard Ivan utter under his breath as he passed by. Alexei clutched his side in pain as he rolled over, afraid of knowing if the wound had split back open.

"Ivan!" Officer Dupont made his way across the yard. "Intolérable!" He looked over at Alexei before continuing. "You will be on guard duty this evening as well as overnight. No breaks, no rest." Looking up, he could see Ivan's face was red with anger.

"Oui, Monsieur!" Ivan shouted, making his way back to the front of the yard along with the others.

"Are you all right?" Dupont made his way over as Alexei attempted to stand.

"I think so." He stood up and brushed off his pants, attempting to ignore the pain in his side. "He just knocked the wind out of me."

"Very good." Dupont placed a hand on his shoulder. "It would be a shame for you to die on your first day of drills." He smiled at him, and Alexei smiled back in return, appreciating the humor.

Returning to the front, Dupont said something that Alexei couldn't quite make out, but from the actions of everyone else moving back inside, it seemed as if he had dismissed everyone. As the soldiers returned inside, he noticed that Ivan was still glaring at him. He wasn't sure what to make of Ivan. His curiosity had only seemed to stem anger and hatred, but he had no idea as to why.

Suddenly, another twinge of pain shot across his ribs.

"Lexi! Are you all right?" He heard Reggie's voice echo from the other side of the yard. Running over, he approached the other officer.

"A little roughhousing by a fellow soldier, it seems." Dupont stated, glaring right at Ivan.

Grabbing his side, Alexei squinted his eyes to manage. "I

will be fine. I think I just need to take a break."

Reggie walked up to him and took his arm. "Come. Let's get you upstairs." With that, Reggie led him through the hall and back to the stairwell in front of the house. "Are you able to walk up?" Alexei nodded and proceeded to climb the stairs slowly. Once at the top, they made their way to the bedroom. Reggie grabbed the door and opened it, allowing Alexei to enter and make his way to the bed. "I will grab you some water and bandages if you need them." He left down the hall towards the washroom as Alexei began to open the buttons of his jacket, revealing his white buttoned shirt underneath. So far, he did not see any sign of blood. The bandage seemed to be holding tight.

When Reggie returned, he had a pitcher of water in his hand as well as another roll of bandage and tape. He closed the door and made his way over to the bed. As Alexei began unbuttoning his white shirt, Reggie noticed the bandage that was already affixed to his skin. "I didn't realize you were already hurt." He said staring at the wound.

Undoing the last button, Alexei slipped off the shirt. "It is from that night..." That night had been a little over a week ago now. He thought it was strange how time had flown by, yet his wound remained, albeit a little better than it was at the beginning. "When the shots rang out, I felt one of them hit me in the ribs. Luckily, my sisters' plan of sewing the jewels did the trick of stopping the bullet, but it caused one of the jewels to pierce my skin." Opening the bandage, he could see redness around the wound, but no blood, which was a relief.

"That must have been a difficult thing to see, Lexi. I'm sorry you went through that." A part of Reggie had opened up to him. Something he had not seen before. Up to this point, he had been a very confident, yet sometimes immature, young man. Now, he could see a sorrowful gaze, almost one of pity, and he wasn't sure how to feel.

"I am glad to be alive, Reggie. I just wish the others...my family...were alive as well." Fully peeling off the bandage, Reggie handed him a cloth to wipe around it, followed by another bandage and tape.

"I see you are pretty good at taking care of yourself." Reggie sat down on the bed across from him. "Hell, if the world knew where you were right now, others might see you in a completely different light."

Placing the bandage on the wound caused him to squirm a little. "By 'others', you mean those from my country?" He placed the tape on the bandage to seal it up. "I think they would like nothing more than to see me lying next to my father."

"The Bolsheviks, maybe." Reggie leaned back against the wall, propping his feet up. "Surely the rest of Russia would see the wrong that was done."

"I fear by then it will be too late." Finishing the bandage, Alexei moved in a parallel position on his bed, facing Reggie. "Who knows what will happen when the rest of the world knows about this."

Reggie glanced out the window. "Have you thought about an alternative life?" Alexei gazed at him as his focus remained outside. "You know, start over with a new name and everything. Surely, they would never find you then."

He took a breath before responding. "I do not wish to be made a coward." That statement seemed to sadden Reggie, his attention slowly turning back towards the room. "If I am to live, I want to be allowed to live as I am. My father has abdicated the throne, and the Bolsheviks have obtained power. I do not know if there is anything to go home to, but I will not be shoved into a closet and made to be forgotten. The world deserves to know the truth of my family, and what cruel and heinous things were done to them, all the way up until their final moments."

"You are a brave one." Reggie was now looking directly at him. "I don't know that I could say the same, should something ever happen like that to my family." He hung his head for a moment. "Perhaps that makes me a coward."

Alexei shook his head. "I do not believe it makes you a coward." He saw a hint of a smirk on Reggie's face. "Everyone's journey is different in this world. The way we navigate it is our own. Courage can be bold but can also be dangerous. Sometimes it is best to put courage aside for safety's sake. You might find you come out alive on the other end...albeit alone." Alexei followed suit by hanging his head.

"But you are not alone, Lexi." His eyes glared up at Reggie, who was now staring at him from across the room. "Luka and Klara protected you while you were in their care. Luka brought you here, knowing full well that it could mean his life. He brought you to me, hoping that there was something I could do. When he first contacted me, I didn't believe him. He knew that I was stationed here in Nice, training soldiers and sending them off to war. He thought that I would be able to help you, or at least harbor you until we could figure out the next step. And that's exactly what we did." He looked away for a moment. "Your life means more to the world than you might know, Lexi. Don't take that for granted."

A tear began to run down Alexei's cheek as he brushed it away. "Thank you, Reggie. I should hope to return the favor one day." Thinking for a moment, he slid off the bed and looked around for his satchel. Reaching inside, he grabbed the small sack that sat at the bottom. Walking over to Reggie, he grabbed a handful of the jewels. He chose three and placed the rest back into the sack.

The jewels were two different colors, one red, and two blue. Picking up the red one, he handed it to Reggie. "I want you to have this." He placed the jewel in his hand. "It is a symbol of my commitment to you and your friends and family and a symbol of our friendship." Reggie smiled as he clasped his hand around the jewel. He held out the blue jewels for him to take as well, but Reggie hesitated. "These two jewels are for Luka and Klara. I ask that you deliver them when you see them next, as I'm sure you will see them before I do." Reggie's hand opened to receive the two blue jewels.

"You know I could sell these?" Reggie's comment made him smirk.

"Then how will the world ever know that you were truly

friends with a real prince? You would lose your bragging rights." He laughed a little, as did Reggie.

The remainder of the day, Reggie stopped by his room several times to check on him, making sure that he had food and plenty of rest. He spent the afternoon and evening browsing newspapers and journals from the last day or so, but couldn't seem to find anything interesting, all seeming to be old news recycled into new stories. By the time the sun had set, his eyes were so blurry from reading that he couldn't see in front of him, so he decided to call it for the night.

Reggie, Luka, and Klara had all been kind to him this last week. Their generosity made him feel for a brief period like the world was realigning in his favor.

17

"Hurry children!" His father said, fixing his navy jacket as the guards led them down the hallway. Alexei had fallen a few steps behind Anastasia, his youngest sister, who had taken notice and stopped to grab his hand.

"Come along, everything is going to be fine." she said in a hushed tone. He looked at her and smiled briefly, a feeling of déjà vu and a sense of dread surrounding him as he followed her.

His father, Nicholas, glanced over at him briefly before continuing down the dark hallway. Over the last few months, he watched his father age greatly. Grey hairs sprouting from his mustache and the top of his head, wrinkles appearing across his face, and the absence of any glee had added at least fifteen years to the middle-aged man's face. The look he adorned for the last several weeks was one of worry, and it never seemed to change.

Beside his father walked his mother, Alexandra. She had always been a strong individual, leading the household firmly whenever his father was out at military training or seeing to country negotiations. Her firm hand in the family aided in shaping his sisters' personalities, but her personality seemed to get her into trouble. After his father left to lead troops in the war, his mother took over negotiations at home, and the people of Russia did not seem to like the granddaughter of Queen Victoria leading them. Nevertheless, she forged on to give sovereign advice and counsel whenever needed.

His eldest sister, Olga, walked alongside his mother, her head hanging low as if her fate had already been sealed. *Her fate...his fate...he was certain he had been here before*. Olga had taken after their mother in almost every way, including trying to protect him from getting hurt. But over the last few months, her demeanor had changed into an almost nonchalant tone.

Then there was Tatiana, the second oldest. One of her favorite pieces of clothing that she wore every day was her white headband. She always said it aided in keeping her wild hair out of her eyes. Alexei had always laughed at Tatiana's jokes, as she was more quick-witted than the rest of the family. He always wished he could come up with things to say as fast as she did.

After Tatiana was his second youngest sister, Maria, who was only five years older than him, but they never really connected as siblings. Moreover, Maria would spend most of her time outside the palace, galivanting with soldiers and townspeople as often as she could. Their mother had tried to rein her in at one point, but Alexei felt it just made matters worse. Even during the imprisonment... *wait... they were being held captive*. Maria would sneak off and talk to the soldiers who were maintaining post at their door, attempting to flirt but unsure of what she would gain. Now, she walked as if on a mission, unlike the rest of the family.

Finally, holding onto his hand was his youngest sister, Anastasia. Older than him by three years, the two had grown exceedingly attached over the years. At times, the girls would be called away for a ceremony outside of the palace, but Anastasia would choose to stay to be with her little brother. Their bond had always been something he knew that his other sisters had admired but would never have. Her hand tightly held his as they paraded down the dark hallway toward a barely lit wooden door.

Suddenly, it dawned on him. This was it... the moments before he and his family were to be shuffled into a basement and shot to death by Bolshevik soldiers. His palms grew sweaty, and he could feel himself starting to go numb. He had to say something to his father quickly, while the guards were scarce.

"You're cold." He heard Anastasia say to him as she peered at his face. "You look sick, brother."

He shook his head as he let go of her hand. "I must get to Father." For a second, he started to push forward, attempting to grab the Tsar's attention. "Father." he said quietly, but Nicholas didn't seem to notice. A louder voice came. "Father!"

Nicholas turned his head to see his son, attempting to get to the front. He turned and reached out his hand, and Alexei took it, bringing himself closer to the front of the group.

"Father, I have to tell you something." His voice sounded desperate.

His father responded calmly. "It will have to wait, my dear boy. We are going to be saved tonight. You will have plenty of time to tell me afterward."

Saved? What does he mean by that?

"No, Father. I don't think you understand..." Alexei tried to remain calm. "They do not intend to save us."

His father looked at him strangely. "What on earth do you mean, my son?"

He took a breath. "They are going to kill us. All of us."

With a face filled with shock, his father yanked Alexei closer to him. "And how do you know of such a thing?"

Another deep breath. "You just have to trust me."

"What is going on up there?!" He heard the guard yell from behind them.

Suddenly, his father stopped the group from walking further. "We must wait a moment. My son has injured himself and needs to be mended."

The guard grunted in response. "No time for foolishness. Keep moving!"

Without hesitation, his father yelled. "Get their guns!"

Before he knew it, his father had apprehended the gun from the guard in the front, seemingly knocking him unconscious, as the guard in the back was being wrestled by Alexei's two eldest sisters. He eventually swung them away, but not before his father could point the gun at him, forcing him to raise his hands and drop the weapon on the ground. "You will pay for this. You all will die before this night has ended. You have my word."

"We shall see about that." His father stated forcefully.

More noises could be heard coming from the other side of the long hallway. The soldiers and guards had heard the commotion and began to file down to inspect the area. Nicholas looked around for a moment. "Quick, everyone inside." He opened a door and ushered the family inside a room one by one. But, as he was shutting the door, a powerful force pushed on it, causing it to burst open. Hordes of guards swarmed the room, surrounding his family with their guns drawn.

"You should not be so much trouble, Nicholas." A man walked into the room, adorned with metals and pins on his jacket, much more than an average soldier. "This only makes matters more complicated."

His three oldest sisters began to sob, while his mother remained as stone-faced as she had been before. Anastasia looked right at him, her face full of fear. "How did you know?"

"Silence!" The decorated soldier shouted. Reaching into his jacket pocket, he pulled out a small postcard and began to read the text. "Nikolai Alexandrovich, in view of the fact that your relatives are continuing their attack on Soviet Russia, the Ural Executive Committee has decided to execute you."

Alexei's ears began ringing, and suddenly his head was filled with the screams of his family.

"Lexi?"

He closed his eyes, hoping that he could have another chance to try again. Perhaps he could save them if only he could go back.

"Lexi. Come on."

Slowly opening his eyes, he saw a pistol aimed right at his head, and he flinched before hearing the gunshot.

"Lexi! Wake up!"

A slight scream jolted him awake and startled Reggie, who was sitting next to him. For a few seconds, they looked at each other, unsure of what to say next. Alexei composed himself. "I apologize. I…had a bad dream."

Reggie appeared concerned, shaking his head. "It's okay."

Looking at the clock on the nightstand, he noticed it was still nighttime. "Reggie, it's almost midnight. Why are you waking me up this late?"

Turning his head towards the window, Alexei could see Reggie's face illuminated by the moon. He seemed to have a satchel on his back. "We're leaving tonight for Paris. Get up and get packed. LeBlanc is waiting for us outside."

18

It only took Alexei a few minutes to get everything packed and ready to go. His satchel had been kept securely underneath his bed, trying to keep anyone from snooping when they were around. The only thing he had left to do was put on his green vest and lace up his boots. Reggie waited for him by the door, anxiously watching as he finished tying his bootlaces.

"Reggie." Alexei caught his attention. "You said that 'we' are leaving tonight. Are you planning on going with us now?"

Pushing himself off the door frame, Reggie replied. "Yes, but I can only go as far as Paris, you know that." Alexei sighed slightly. "We can't take any risks of suspicion. If spies are lurking around, two French soldiers crossing the border with a teenage boy is bound to catch some attention." Reggie walked up to him and placed his hand on his shoulder. "But don't worry, you are safe so long as you are with us, Lexi. I promise."

"I believe you. I am also glad that you will be coming with us to Paris." Finishing the last lace, he swung his satchel around his shoulder. "There. I'm ready."

"Bon!" Reggie responded, moving towards the door. Hearing the hinges creak, he poked his head out to look for anyone who might be awake, then motioned for Alexei to follow him. "Are you feeling better since this afternoon?" he asked quietly as they entered the hallway towards the stairwell.

"I am, thank you." They both smiled as they began to descend the stairs. Quietly, their footsteps made little to no sound with each step they took. Reaching the bottom, Reggie pointed towards the front door, motioning him to move towards it. Alexei obeyed and began to make his way forward, stopping to look left and right every few steps to make sure no one was watching him.

Upon reaching the front door, he turned the knob slowly until he heard a click. The door opened much easier than he had remembered from a few days ago when he had first entered with Luka. He hadn't been out of the front door since.

Poking his head outside, he noticed a shadowed figure leaning up against a light post across the street. Tilting his head towards the light, he could see that it was General LeBlanc, looking as composed as he had been the day before. There were so many questions Alexei wanted to ask him, especially with how quickly he was able to get everything situated, but there wasn't any time for that. Getting to Paris safely was the primary focus.

Walking across the street, Alexei tried to keep his head down as he made his way toward LeBlanc.

"Is Reggie still joining us?" LeBlanc asked in a monotone voice.

"Yes." A one-word response was simple enough to answer the General's question, to which he responded with a simple nod.

Hearing the door to the house shut behind him, Alexei looked around to see Reggie making his way toward them, his facial expression showing as if they were getting ready to go on a holiday.

"Very good." LeBlanc uttered softly as Reggie approached. "Now, our train leaves in twenty minutes. We will get there in just enough time for it to take off. We don't want to be sitting around waiting for the departure. We will talk more about Paris once we're on board. Reggie, should anything happen, you are to take command and see that the crown prince gets to London."

Imitating a sailor, Reggie responded. "Aye, aye, cap'n!"

LeBlanc rolled his eyes. "All right then, let's be off." Turning in the direction of the train station, they began to walk, with Alexei in the middle.

Turning back one more time to see the house, he was able to get a better look before they turned the corner. Looking at the window of his room, he could tell that he left the light on, illuminating the corner of the room. All the other windows were dark, but one of them seemed off. Staring more intently, Alexei could make out a shadow in the darkness, as if someone had noticed them leaving. He stared for another moment to try to get his eyes to adjust, when it finally hit him who was there. Ivan, the tormentor, spotting a captain, a general, and a recruit leaving in the dead of night. Alexei wondered if he should say something to Reggie, but instead chose to keep quiet, and focused a few more seconds on Ivan's face. He could sense the rage from outside and it sent a chill up his spine. Turning the corner, Ivan's face disappeared, as did the window and the house entirely.

LeBlanc kept a steady speed, forcing Alexei to move a little quicker than usual. Keeping his head forward, he motioned them through the next few streets. Reggie followed close behind, closing the gap between the two of them whenever he felt he was too far away. The darkness surrounded them for much of the walk, except for the occasional streetlight, illuminating them briefly.

Turning another corner, Alexei could finally see the lights of the train station. It was evening the last time he saw it when Luka had brought him here from Russia, but it looked much prettier in the dark as the lamps inside illuminated the station in an almost comforting feeling. He could see that there were only a couple of people inside, a conductor and a ticket taker. Both seemed like they were waiting for their arrival.

Upon entering the train station, LeBlanc approached the ticket taker and presented him with three tickets from his left jacket pocket. The ticket taker glanced at the tickets before returning them and motioning them onward toward the station.

Inside, the conductor stood next to a seemingly empty train, anxiously awaiting their arrival.

"Bonsoir, Général." The man said in a nervous voice. They met each other's gaze for a moment only for the conductor to nod and instantly look at Reggie. "Officer Bellion."

Alexei looked around as LeBlanc began to board. "Are we the only ones on this train?" He began to feel sweat beading on his forehead.

Turning around, LeBlanc looked at him. "It's a midnight train. Almost no one rides these if they can help it." From the look on the conductor's face, it appeared as if LeBlanc had found a way to secure privacy on this coach. Instead of questioning further, he relented and followed him onboard the train.

They entered the first car, showcasing a line of private cabins, followed by what appeared to be the dining car. Sliding open the first door of the private cabin at the front of the train, LeBlanc entered as Alexei and Reggie followed. Once inside, Reggie slid the door closed and threw his bag onto one of the red cushioned seats. LeBlanc followed suit and Alexei felt compelled to do the same.

Moving towards the window, Reggie sat down on the cushioned seat and motioned for Alexei to join him. He walked over and sat beside him, looking out the window to see the night sky and stars glimmering above. LeBlanc sat across from them and took a deep breath.

"All aboard!" the conductor shouted, closing the train car door behind him, and moving toward the front.

Reggie adjusted in his seat. "So, it truly is just us." He looked at Alexei. "Sorry, you won't be getting your big party tonight." He grinned, causing Alexei to laugh slightly.

"We only have a few hours until we arrive in Paris." LeBlanc's monotone voice attempted to take control of the room again. "Let us make sure we talk through the plan."

The train car jolted, and everything outside appeared as if it was starting to move backward. Slowly, the train gained speed before they were out of the station and on their way to Paris.

Alexei glanced up at the stone-faced man sitting across from him. "General LeBlanc, I am ready to discuss your plan." He peered over at Reggie, who had given him a nod of approval.

"Very good." Pulling a rolled cigar from his pocket, LeBlanc took a match and ignited it, puffing at the cigarette until an orange light illuminated the end. "Once we arrive in Paris, we'll need to secure the next train." He put out the match and placed it into a metal holding tray on the ledge of the window. "The crown prince and I will make our way to the platform as soon as the train stops. Our tickets will see us to London through the trains and the ferry so there is no need to revisit the ticket booth." He took another puff of his cigar as he continued. "Reggie, there is a woman in Paris that I need you to send a message to for me." Reaching into his left coat pocket, he pulled out a sealed envelope and handed it to Reggie. "She does not know of our situation, but she is aware that I am passing through and she will be heartbroken if I do not stop to see her or at least give her a sign that I was there."

"Of course. I will ensure that it is delivered." Reggie placed the envelope in his jacket pocket. Alexei was surprised that he didn't pry more on the subject, even though he was curious about who LeBlanc might have been talking about. He speculated that it could have been the royal family member Reggie had been referring to a few days prior, the one that LeBlanc had supposedly been seeing.

"Thank you, Reggie." LeBlanc turned his attention back to Alexei. "Now, once we are on board the train for London, we will need to keep a low profile. Paris and Nice are two different beasts. If anyone is looking for you, they'll be looking in Paris." Alexei grabbed for his satchel and took out his hat, showing it to the general. "Already prepared, I see. Yes, you'll want to hide your face, if possible." He took another puff of his cigar. "Once we are moving on the London train, we should be safe. Sergeant Blackwell will be waiting for us at the arrival platform there. He will assume your safety at that time, and I will return to Paris."

"Will I be meeting with Cousin George?" Alexei interrupted, his face anticipating the answer.

"I...cannot say for certain." He took the cigar out of his mouth and frowned. "I did not get a chance to clear that up with Thomas when we last spoke." Alexei let his face droop towards the floor, clutching his hat in his hands. "That does not mean that it isn't happening, I just do not have the knowledge to provide you an answer."

"I...understand." Alexei lifted his head and nodded at LeBlanc. What he had wanted was an answer, something that would have let him know if his extended relatives had betrayed his family at any point during the war, but it didn't seem he was going to get that answer, at least not tonight. Instead, he tilted his head to look past Reggie and out of the window, watching as the dark trees and flickering lights in the night sky passed him by.

"Let's get some rest." LeBlanc said, lowering the shade on the windows. "While we still have a few more hours of guaranteed peace."

19

Peeling his eyes open, Alexei wondered how long he had been asleep. The shades still shrouded the darkness of the night sky as he shuffled himself into an upright position. Opposite him, LeBlanc lay still with his eyes closed, resting his head against the back of the seat rest, his mouth hanging agape, and a slight snoring sound muttered out of it. Adjusting his shoulders, he looked to his left and noticed Reggie was not beside him. Pulling himself together, he stood up and made his way for the cabin door.

The train was eerily quiet. It moved along at such a fast speed that the constant noise of the train wheels and tracks blended into the background. Sliding open the door, he stepped into the dimly illuminated hallway, appearing to only be lit by a few light bulbs in each car. He looked down each section of the hall to see if he could spot Reggie, but he did not see him. He felt the door slide shut behind him as he turned and made his way to the back of the car.

As he approached, he noticed the next train car appeared

to be empty, except for a few tables and chairs and a sitting bar that looked outside. On a stool at the far end of the bar sat Reggie, one hand propping up his head as he fought to stay awake. Alexei opened the door to the car and entered, causing Reggie to take notice of him.

"Ah, so the young prince is awake." Reggie said with a grin. "Don't like to be caught sleeping in anymore, eh?" Alexei approached, taking the stool next to him.

"Remember Reggie, titles are not a thing that I enjoy, especially from those that know me." He stared sternly at him for a second before cracking a smile.

"Heh, of course, Lexi." Looking back out the window, Reggie stared into the darkness for a few moments. "You know, before joining the war, I would have never thought of myself in the position that I am in right now. An aspirant, assisting royalty in escaping their homeland, merely using France as a buffer zone. It's all out of some story, it seems."

Alexei's fingers tapped on the bar. "Do you regret..." He hung his head again.

Reggie quickly interjected. "Oh God, no! In fact, I wouldn't trade it! This has been an exhilarating adventure thus far." He took a drink from a glass to his right before placing it back down on the bar.

"What about your family, Reggie? I mean, besides Luka and Klara." Alexei watched as Reggie's face sank.

"My mother died when I was young. I barely even remember her. My father raised me, scraping together everything he could to make sure that we could get by. He worked two jobs to ensure that I could go to the best school around. He was an amazing father." He took another drink. "Then, the war came four years ago, and everything changed. My father moved to Paris to be closer to his own extended family, but I wanted to remain in Reims, and so I stayed, at nineteen, and my father left. He wrote a few times, and I did go to visit twice during his stay there. The last time I visited with him was early in March, three years ago." He went quiet for a moment.

"What happened?" Alexei asked, watching as Reggie took another drink from his glass.

"Three days after I departed back for Reims, Paris was bombed by a German Zeppelin. I tried for days to get ahold of my father, or anyone who might have seen him, but it was no use. Then, I phoned the police, and they checked my father's name against a register that they were keeping of those found in the bombing, and his name was on it, identified by a small sliver of note in his wallet." A tear began to form in his left eye. "Afterwards, Luka and Klara journeyed from Russia to see me, and to make sure that I was doing well. Luka was my mother's older brother and had always helped my father whenever he could when it came to raising me. I told them my intentions, of how I wanted to join the war to avenge my father and all those that had died at the hands of this war. Klara tried to talk me out of it, but Luka never said a word. Instead, he placed his hand on my shoulder and told me that he would support me no matter what decision I made." He wiped the tear from his eye.

"Reggie, I'm so sorry." Alexei placed his hand on Reggie's back. "Our stories aren't so different, you know?" Reggie looked at him peculiarly. "We've both experienced a great loss throughout our young lives."

Reggie nodded. "Yes, that is true." He glanced over at his drink, which was now empty. "But yours is a worse tragedy, I feel. I don't know if I would have reacted as you did if I was thirteen at the time." He placed his hand on Alexei's shoulder. "You are very brave, and I hope our journey together is not over after tonight." Both smiled at each other, Alexei nodding in agreement.

Hearing the door open behind them, they turned to see LeBlanc entering. They dropped their hands to their sides as he approached.

"We're close to Paris." LeBlanc's monotone voice seemed even deeper after waking up. He pointed out the window, noting the faint flicker of lights in the distance. "We'll want to start getting ready. This switch needs to be swift."

"Right." Alexei said as LeBlanc made his way back towards the cabin. Reggie stood up from his stool and began to follow. "Reggie?" He turned to notice Alexei. "Thank you for sharing your story with me. It truly means a lot."

Reggie nodded. "Thank you for listening." He reached into his pocket and pulled out the red jewel that Alexei had given him the previous day. "And thank you for trusting me."

Alexei smiled.

20

With his satchel secured, Alexei watched as the other two men finished preparing themselves for the train's arrival in Paris. Outside, the lights grew brighter as they approached the city. A few lights here and there suddenly turned into a mass of illumination in front of his eyes. He looked over to see Reggie strapping his sack to his back and LeBlanc holstering and securing his gun to his side.

The train began to slow as the outside world became brighter. LeBlanc grabbed his bag and tossed it onto his back before turning to Reggie. "Ready?" With a stern nod, he turned to look at Alexei, who nodded sternly in response.

Grabbing his black hat, he placed it on his head, just as he did the night they escaped from Yekaterinburg. He attempted to shield his face as much as possible with the bill of the flat cap, knowing that any slight turn upward would prove him noticeable.

LeBlanc slid the door open to the main car, and the three exited the cabin. Standing by the train door, Reggie shifted slightly, as if nerves had begun to creep in.

"You remember your orders?" LeBlanc asked Reggie, as he glanced back at him. "The letter."

"Yes, I remember." Reggie patted his left jacket pocket to signify where the letter was kept. "I will see you two to the train first." His eyes shifted to Alexei. "It's the least I can do before we part ways." Alexei smiled.

LeBlanc sighed. "Very well." The train slowed as the outside view seemed to enter a large building. More people stood outside this time, seemingly waiting for a train of their own. "You must remember that it is morning. There will be more people traveling the train at this hour. Be on your guard." He patted his holstered gun for reassurance.

As the train came to a stop, groups of people began to congregate around the train doors, causing Alexei to feel anxious. His palms began to sweat, and his breath got heavy. Suddenly, a hand rested on his shoulder. He looked over to see Reggie giving him a slight grin. He returned the grin and placed his head back down into the shadow of his hat.

The conductor appeared outside the train car, motioning people to get back as he opened the door for the group to exit. All at once, the door opened, and a rush of people began to make their way into the car. About twenty people pushed past the three as they made their way out, some even knocking into them as they tried to exit.

"Eh, watch it, will ye!?" A voice shouted from the mixed crowd of people. Alexei tried not to pay any attention to those entering and focused on LeBlanc making his way out of the train. Finally, the three were able to push their way out onto the platform.

LeBlanc looked around for a moment before pointing in a direction and began walking immediately. "This way."

Reggie and Alexei followed close behind, hordes of people still fighting to get to their train. Alexei felt dizzy for a moment, the world seemingly spinning around him. The people walking past him hastily made his stomach queasy. It wasn't until Reggie grabbed his arm that he realized he had stopped in the middle of the platform. He shook his head and began to walk again, catching up with LeBlanc as he made his way forward.

All the people seemed to come out of nowhere. Twenty people turned into forty; forty turned into a hundred. Everything happened so fast. Alexei lifted his hat briefly to look at the train station. A large clock embedded in the wall told him it was almost five in the morning. Train tracks sat on each side of the cement platform as they made their way down. The walls on both sides were painted white but stained with soot.

"Train is here. It's departing soon." He heard from LeBlanc in front of him. His eyes peered around to take in the train station once more before hopping on the train.

A face crossed his vision, which caused him to backtrack. He had seen someone who looked familiar to him, but he wasn't sure if he was simply seeing things. He looked around again, attempting to find the face one more time. Suddenly, his eyes met the recognizable face. The man stood tall, his beard and mustache well-groomed and maintained. He wore a military cap, but Alexei couldn't see the rest of him. For the last year or so, Alexei had seen this man escorting his father wherever he went, making sure he wasn't going to cause trouble. The last time he had seen him was that night in the basement, where his family was murdered, holding a bayonetted rifle. The man's eyes grew wide immediately.

"General!" Alexei shouted to get his attention. They had just reached the next train and were getting ready to board when LeBlanc turned to face him. "There's a man here. A man that knows who I am. He saw me."

"Merde!" LeBlanc cursed as he ushered Alexei onto the train. Reggie looked around, trying to find the man. "What did he look like?"

"Tall, beard and mustache. He was wearing his military cap." Alexei grew nervous. He didn't want to be captured by the Russian army again. He couldn't fathom what they would do to him if they got their hands on him a second time.

"Get to the back of the train." LeBlanc took off his bag and handed it to Alexei. "Head to the back of the train and don't stop until it starts moving."

"All aboard!" The conductor shouted.

With that, LeBlanc made his way back into the crowd of people. Hoisting the bag over his shoulder with his satchel, Alexei turned to make his way toward the back of the train.

"Lexi!" Reggie said, attempting to catch his attention. Alexei turned to face him as he reached for him. With a snap, Reggie snatched the black flat cap off his head. "I need to borrow this." He put the cap on his head. "Be safe, Lexi. We shall meet again one day." With that, Reggie turned and made his way into the crowd as well.

Walking towards the back of the train, Alexei looked out the windows, attempting to find LeBlanc. A few train cars down, the doors were closing as he spotted the familiar man, LeBlanc heading in his direction to catch up. He did not seem to notice him on the train, so Alexei knelt lower to peer out of the window.

The man looked around in a fury, attempting to find any trace of Alexei. LeBlanc got closer, and the mustache man took notice. He could tell that LeBlanc was saying something to him but could not be sure what. Reggie appeared just a few steps behind him, wearing the black flat cap on his head.

In an instant, the man drew his gun, prompting LeBlanc to do the same, but he wasn't quick enough. Seconds seemed like hours as the man fired a gunshot right at LeBlanc, striking him in the chest. LeBlanc fell to the ground as Reggie turned to run. The man followed.

"No!" Alexei shouted. He realized that everyone around him had heard the gunshot as well and had taken notice of the platform where General LeBlanc lay in a pool of his own blood. He tried to look ahead to see Reggie, but the crowd outside had begun to panic and run in all directions.

Another gunshot came from outside, this time near the front of the train. Alexei feared that the shot meant they had gotten Reggie as well. He could not see the black flat cap anymore in the hoard of people.

The train started to move, slowly exiting the station. As it moved, Alexei continued to stare out the window, trying to find any hint of Reggie's fate. The mustached man came into view again, his tall head looking around one more time for a sign of the young prince. Alexei ducked his head underneath the window to shield himself from view.

For a moment, he sat there, thinking about LeBlanc and Reggie, and everything that they had done for him to get him here.

Tears began to pool at the bottom of his eyes and trickle down his cheeks. Reggie had trusted him in the last couple of days, and he had been grateful for the return of friendship. Now, he had let him die for the cause of his safety. Alexei began to wonder if everything he was putting everyone through was worth his safety. Perhaps the world would have been better off if he had perished with his family.

Wiping the tears from his eyes, he peered out the window to see the night sky again. They had exited the train station. He stood up and made his way towards the second to last train car.

As the door opened, a few people stood while others sat, still discussing the gunfire they heard at the station. Many people seemed rattled by the event as he walked past them. Grown men were comforting each other as women held their children. These people had been through so much in the last few years. From the bombings to the deaths of their men on the battlefield, the Allies had seen so much darkness. Alexei prayed there would soon be a light at the end of the tunnel, and that this war would come to an end.

Finding a seat, Alexei slung the two bags on the ground and sat down. All he could think about were Reggie and LeBlanc and how they had fought to save his life. Senseless bloodshed over a power struggle in his own country, which bled into other countries.

He wondered if he would ever be safe. Would the resistance forever try to hunt him down? If they were to capture him again, surely they wouldn't let him live long enough to make a plea. If he made it to Great Britain, would Cousin George grant him refuge?

Thoughts raced through his mind as he sat back in his seat, looking outside as the sun began to rise slowly on the eastern skyline. A new day had arrived, and the safety he had felt over the last few days was completely shattered. Once again, he felt like a vulnerable thirteen-year-old boy, unsure of what to do next.

Reaching for his bag, Alexei pulled out the small sack with the jewels inside. He had entrusted Reggie with three jewels: one for him, and one each for Luka and Klara. If Reggie was killed, those jewels will never reach their destination. For a moment, he felt guilty he had not given a jewel to LeBlanc.

He massaged the sack in his hand for a few more seconds before placing it back into his satchel. Looking out the window, the sunbeams began bursting through the skyline to call the morning. He sat there and stared as the sun broke through, trying his hardest not to feel alone again.

21

The next few hours crawled by as Alexei stared out the window, watching the sun rise fully into the sky. By the time the train had reached the French border, it was already early afternoon. He peered around every so often to see if anyone had noticed him, but none seemed to give him a second glance. He was thankful for that.

Upon arriving in the port city of Calais, exiting the train and boarding the ferry took almost no time at all. Alexei attempted to keep his head down the entire voyage across the water, refraining from looking at anyone in fear that someone might notice him. Reboarding the next train was easy to board right off the ferry in Dover after entering the United Kingdom. From there, it was only another few hours until London finally came into view.

To his right sat his satchel, as well as LeBlanc's bag he had given to him before he chased after the mustached man. The sack of jewels had been tucked away in his satchel, but he became curious as to what might have been in LeBlanc's bag.

Reaching over, he grabbed it and sat it on his lap, staring at it for a few moments before flipping open the flap and pulling the drawstring loose.

Inside, Alexei noticed a change of clothes as well as a travel case filled with a razor, spare razorblades, tweezers, a toothbrush, and a shaving bar. All the items looked as if they had never been used. He took the travel case out and examined the leather. Being only thirteen, he hadn't seen much need for a razor, but the toothbrush was a welcomed addition to his satchel. Placing the travel case back into the General's bag, he saw a small envelope at the bottom. He tugged it free from underneath the clothes and read the front, 'Sergeant Blackwell' in black ink. Turning the envelope over, he noticed that it wasn't sealed. Flipping open the lip, he took the letter out and unfolded it, taking a moment to read what had been written down.

'Dear Thomas,

If this letter makes it your way, then that means that trouble has arisen between Paris and London, and I am not able to accompany the boy any further. Please see him safely to his next destination. I will make contact as soon as I can, although this letter may cause you to fear the worst. The boy still wishes to see King George, hopefully, you were able to make proper arrangements. I trust that your plan will be effective. Until we speak again.

Général Hugo LeBlanc'

Placing the letter back into the envelope, Alexei stared at the writing. He wondered what Sergeant Blackwell had planned once he arrived in London. Alexei couldn't think of anything except for meeting with Cousin George and being granted asylum, but he wasn't sure of the chances of that happening. Still, he held out hope as he placed the envelope in his vest pocket. Tightening the drawstring on the bag, he flipped the leather flap back over and placed it beside him.

Another ten minutes passed until he started seeing

buildings on both sides of the train, followed by the sound of the gears grinding. He had finally made it to London. Now, all he needed to do was get off the train successfully and find Sergeant Blackwell. Where would he be waiting though? And how would he know what he looked like? These questions floated through his head as the train entered the station.

The train station was much bigger than most of the others he had seen, almost as big as the one in St. Petersburg where he had spent most of his childhood. The brick façade showed signs of wear and tear but was mostly intact.

As the train slowed, Alexei grabbed both bags and began to make his way toward the doors of the train. Once the train stopped, he noticed the conductor, along with three other men coming down the line to open doors for the passengers. Outside, a huge flock of people waited to enter, almost as many as he had seen in Paris.

The door opened and he quickly made his way into the station, looking around as others struggled to push past him. On the other side of the station was an open area, mostly for patrons of the coffee shops to sit and drink while they read their papers. He decided to head in that direction.

Finding a seat, he sat down at one of the tables under a shop that read "Café au Lait", a simple name for a coffee shop. For a moment, he looked around to see if he could spot someone looking for another person without making himself look too obvious. He decided to make himself comfortable and took a moment to breathe deeply.

"Ey now." He heard a woman's voice from behind him. "If you're gonna sit here, you gotta order somethin'." Turning his head, he noticed the woman staring at him. Her bulky frame and stern face looked as if she could command a whole fleet of ships, never mind a coffee shop.

A moment passed, and Alexei stood up. "I deeply apologize." He nodded towards the woman, grabbing his bags. "I do not have any money to offer."

The woman grunted. "I think your hearing is a bit off."

His head tilted in her direction. "I'm sorry?"

"I didn't ask if you had any money. I said you gotta order somethin'. Now why don't you sit back down." Her speech felt like a command, and so he obeyed. "Very good. Now, how about a pasty and some coffee? It's not much, but it's a start." She stared at him intently, her deep brown eyes matching her chestnut hair.

Alexei nodded. "That...sounds lovely, miss. Thank you for your generosity." Instead of responding, she turned and walked back towards her shop. He took another deep breath.

A few more minutes passed until the woman returned, holding a coffee cup and a pasty on a plate. "Here you are now. Eat up, and then you'll see yourself off." Alexei nodded and began to devour the food in front of him, occasionally stopping to take a swig of the room-temperature coffee she had given him. He didn't think he looked like a beggar, but something he had done or said must have made the woman take pity on him. As much as he disliked being a charity cause, he was grateful for her kindness.

He had just finished the last few bites of his food when he heard footsteps approaching from behind. Thinking that the woman was coming back to escort him out, he stood up quickly and grabbed his bags.

"Alexei?" Hearing his name out loud sent a shiver down his spine. He wasn't sure how to react at first, so he stood still, seemingly frozen in time. Suddenly, a man appeared in front of him, his tall demeanor and military uniform gave him cause for pause, but his red beard assured Alexei he wasn't someone he had met before. "My apologies for startling you. I am Sergeant Thomas Blackwell. I am to meet with..."

"General LeBlanc." Alexei stated, hanging his head.

"Why, yes. So, it is you." Sergeant Blackwell glanced at him for a moment, looking him up and down before looking around. His tone and demeanor seemed softer than LeBlanc's, but Alexei could still see the sincerity in his eyes as they looked back at him. "But, if you're here...where is..."

Reaching into his vest pocket, Alexei pulled out the letter and handed it to Sergeant Blackwell. Taking the letter in his hands, he opened and read it, his blank expression turned into a more sorrowful one.

"So, it seems that Hugo had other plans." He folded the paper, placing it back into the envelope before stuffing it into his pocket. He cleared his throat. "No matter..." Looking at Alexei, he reached for one of the bags. "The plan still stands. Come. Let's get you out of here."

"The rebellion soldiers were in Paris. LeBlanc was attacked. That is why he is not with me." Hanging his head even further, Alexei grabbed his satchel.

"I see." Sergeant Blackwell stopped to take in what was just said before responding. "If that's the case, that could mean that those soldiers are on their way here. We should look to leave as soon as you are ready, your royal highness."

Alexei cringed at the title before looking back at him. "Are we to see King George?"

Sergeant Blackwell's face drooped, telling him all he needed to know before he even responded. "Come. I will fill you in on everything in the car."

He shook his head in disappointment, attempting to contain his anger. Looking at the Sergeant, he nodded. "Very well."

22

"I spoke with the advisor to the king yesterday." Sergeant Blackwell began as they drove towards the outskirts of London. The car was a basic black color with two doors, much smaller than the one his family had taken on trips when he was younger. "I was told that the king refuses to grant asylum to any members of the Russian court. He believes that all, except for Nicholas, are still alive and in Russian captivity, which has called into question your legitimacy as well as your presence in the United Kingdom." Grabbing ahold of the steering wheel, Sergeant Blackwell turned onto another road as the tall buildings began to fade into the background. "Still, the plan will remain."

Alexei shook his head in disbelief. "I cannot believe that the king will not meet with me." He shuffled around in his seat for a moment. "After everything that our family has done for him, it is the least he could do."

"Perhaps we might take some time to reconfigure." Looking at Alexei, the sergeant could see that he was not happy.

"What is the plan, then?" Alexei tried to focus on the

matters at hand, clenching his fists at his side. "If the king will not meet with me, then what is my purpose of being here?"

"I'm taking you to an isolated farmhouse where you'll be looked after until we can figure out what to do next. Now that you're in the U.K., it's all about convincing the king to grant you an audience with him. Hopefully through some more conversation, that can be arranged. For now, this is the plan that we must follow." He looked over at Alexei whose fists were still clenched. "I know that this isn't the answer you wanted, nor is it the haven you expected, but you must trust that I will do what is best and that I will continue to meet with the advisor until he grants an audience. The only thing that will take some convincing is showing the king that you are who you say you are."

Shifting in his seat, Alexei thought for a moment before reaching for his bag behind him. He watched as they entered the countryside. To his left was a field littered with livestock and a large amount of farming equipment standing idle by the road. His family had never traveled outside of London when they visited to the United Kingdom, so his fascination began to take over.

A few more minutes passed as they drove deeper into the country. Finally, Sergeant Blackwell turned into a dirt-drive with a long road leading to an old farmhouse. A massive barn stood in the distance with a large mess of cows grouped outside. The farmhouse had a beautiful white exterior with red shingles on top. Five windows surrounded the front door and a chimney rose from the middle. It wasn't as big as the manor house in Nice, but it looked just as cozy.

Pulling up to the house, the Sergeant stopped the car and proceeded to exit it. "This is it." He grabbed LeBlanc's bag and made his way around to the other side to open the door for Alexei. "By the way, they do not know who you are. I would like to keep it that way for now." Alexei nodded in understanding and then proceeded to exit the vehicle.

The wooden front door of the farmhouse opened, and a

middle-aged man stepped out, followed by a woman around the same age. They closed the door and approached the two as they stepped away from the car.

"Sergeant Blackwell. Good to see you." The man shook hands with the Sergeant, his voice raspy and low. He was wearing a white buttoned-down shirt with a pair of suspenders attached to his trousers pulled up over his shoulders. He then noticed that the man was staring at him. "This must be our little helper." He outstretched his hand, and Alexei did the same. "I'm Albert Swinburn, but you can call me Mr. Swinburn." They shook hands.

"Lexi." He responded with a smile. "Nice to meet you."

Turning his head, he looked over at the woman standing next to him. Her reddish hair flowed in the wind, as did her cream-colored dress, her face spotted with freckles. "This is my wife, Dorothy." She nodded, as did Alexei.

"Nice to meet you as well, Miss Dorothy." She smiled at the recognition.

Mr. Swinburn looked at the Sergeant for a moment before speaking. "Well, why don't we get you inside and your bags put down? Then we'll see about getting you something proper to eat."

Following behind the two, Alexei and Sergeant Blackwell made their way inside the house. The interior was just as beautiful as the outside. Many of the rooms seemed to be separated but the foyer allowed room for a chandelier to hang in the center, a staircase laying in front with two doors on both sides, each leading to a different room of the house.

Upstairs, he could hear footsteps, triggering a nervous reaction. His pulse started to race as the sound of the steps moved closer to the stairs. The palms of his hands began to bead with sweat. Suddenly, two young girls' heads peered from around the corner at the top of the stairs.

"Don't you mind them." Mrs. Swinburn said as she placed her hand on his shoulder. "They're just as nervous as you are." She smiled again, then looked up at the girls. "Lily. Violet. Come down and say hello." The two girls looked at each other before descending the stairwell. They didn't seem too sure of what to think about Alexei at first.

Reaching the last step, the first girl, a little redhead about nine years old, looked at him strangely before speaking. "I'm Lilian, but everyone calls me Lily." She curtsied awkwardly before being shoved out of the way by the other girl, a blond who looked to be just a year or so younger.

"And I'm Violet! But everybody calls me Violet." The comment made Alexei chuckle.

"That's because that is your name, cabbage head!" Lily commented, slightly shoving her sister. Both seemed to be wearing the same white dress.

Mrs. Swinburn did not seem amused. "Lily! Don't call your sister such names." Alexei watched as the girls seemed to laugh at each other.

"My name is Alexei, but you can call me Lexi." He smiled at the girls, causing them to blush before turning around and giggling some more.

"Now girls." Mrs. Swinburn said in a serious tone. "Go outside and see to it that the cows don't need to be fed. Go on now!" With that, the girls rushed past Alexei and bolted out the front door, still giggling as they left. Mrs. Swinburn looked over at her husband. "They'll have manners, I just don't know when."

Mr. Swinburn turned to Sergeant Blackwell. "Tommy, why don't you and I discuss our terms in the sitting area while Lexi here takes his bags upstairs to his room? Dorothy, would you make us up some tea?" She nodded in response.

Sergeant Blackwell took LeBlanc's bag off his shoulder and handed it to Alexei. "Sure!" Taking the bag, he watched as the two men entered the room on the left front of the house, closing the door behind them. He looked over at Mrs. Swinburn, who had walked over to the stairwell.

"You'll find your bedroom upstairs. It will be the second door on the left after you get up there. Do you need me to go with you?" She looked at him with a soft expression.

Alexei shook his head. "No, I think I can manage. Thank you." He nodded as she turned to make her way into the kitchen, which was the furthest door on the right. Taking a breath, he took a few steps before reaching the stairs and began his ascent. The floorboards creaked underneath his feet as he took each step. Reaching the top of the stairs he looked both ways to see that it reflected much of the bottom. On the left were two doors and on the right were two doors, with one door in the middle on the other side of the stairs. The middle door appeared to be the washroom as the door was open and he could see a basin just inside.

Making his way to the second door on the left, he reached for the knob and turned it until the latch gave way, opening into a mostly lit room. The area consisted of a bed and nightstand in the far corner and a dresser on the wall closest to the door. A window allowed a substantial amount of light to shine onto the floorboards.

"So, you must be the new kid." A voice echoed from behind him. He turned to his left to see another young boy coming out of the other room. The boy looked at him briefly as he approached. "They didn't tell me I was going to have competition."

Alexei looked confused. "Competition?"

The boy laughed. "Yeah, for being the best-looking fellow on the farm!" He chuckled a moment before extending his hand. "The name's Eli. A pleasure to meet you."

Alexei shook his hand and smiled. "Lexi. I take it your Mr. and Mrs. Swinburn's son?" He looked to be the spitting image of Mr. Swinburn, albeit much younger and with more blonde hair on his head.

Eli shook his head. "Nah, just another daughter who likes to wear trousers." The young man's comment caused Alexei to laugh. He looked to be only a couple of years older than he was. "It's nice to meet you, Lexi. It will be good having another man around the house."

"I am hoping to be as helpful as I can." His smile continued as Eli looked at him.

"Your accent, you're not British?" Eli cocked his head slightly.

"No, Russian." He felt nervous again admitting that, but he hoped that Eli wouldn't notice.

"Russian, eh? It's different. I like it!" He peered over Alexei's shoulder. "Well, Lexi, do you need some help with those bags?" Eli motioned a hand to grab one of the bags.

"I mean, the room is just here. I think I can manage." Alexei grinned.

"Suit yourself!" Eli turned away back toward the stairs. "But don't come crawling to me when you get lost in this massive maze of a house."

"It was nice to meet you, Eli." Alexei said as Eli waved, heading down the stairs toward the foyer.

After taking a few minutes to unpack and get settled, Alexei felt sleepy and decided to lie down for a nap. When he opened his eyes, he wasn't sure how long he had been asleep, but the rays from the sun began to disappear from the window, giving him the feeling that he had slept longer than he wanted.

Shuffling to his feet, he made his way toward the door and into the hallway. He could hear people talking downstairs, laughing, and chatting. It reminded him of his days in the palace, when his family would sit around the table and laugh, telling jokes and talking about frivolous things. He walked towards the stairs and began to make his way down. Noticing the door across from the parlor where Mr. Swinburn and Sergeant Blackwell had entered earlier was open, he could tell that was where the commotion was coming from.

Reaching the doorway, he saw everyone seated around a rectangular dining room table. Mr. Swinburn sat at one end, Sergeant Blackwell to his right. On Mr. Swinburn's left, the two girls sat, and Eli was seated next to the Sergeant. Beside Eli, a seat sat empty. The chair at the opposite end was also empty but was surely for Mrs. Swinburn.

Eli looked up and noticed him. "Hey! He's finally awake! I

thought someone was gonna have to come up there and beat you with a hammer with all that snoring!" He laughed, as did Lily and Violet. Alexei blushed.

Mr. Swinburn turned his attention to Eli. "Elijah! That's no way to speak to our guest."

Eli quickly stopped and hung his head. "Sorry, Father."

Motioning toward the empty seat next to Eli, Mr. Swinburn spoke again. "Have a seat, Lexi. Dorothy is just bringing in the last of the food."

Entering with a large bowl in her hands, Mrs. Swinburn placed the bowl on the table in front of the group. The bowl looked to contain some type of pie. To the left sat a bowl of vegetable soup as well as some toast. Each chair had a glass filled with water.

Mrs. Swinburn sat down, and the meal commenced. Upon digging into the pie, Alexei could tell it was filled with some type of floured meat. He took a couple of helpings and passed it around, along with the vegetable soup and toast.

During the meal, almost everyone was quiet except for Lily and Violet, who seemed to want to play with their food more than eat it. Eventually Violet shouted, "I hate meat pudding!" referring to the pie that sat in front of them. Everyone seemed to laugh off her rant and kept eating.

After dinner, the girls assisted Mrs. Swinburn with the dishes and Eli went upstairs. Sergeant Blackwell and Mr. Swinburn remained downstairs as the Sergeant was getting ready to say his goodbyes to the family.

Alexei ran back upstairs quickly and then back down as the Sergeant began to leave through the front door.

"Sergeant!" Alexei yelled to get his attention. Sergeant Blackwell turned around. "You said earlier that you needed something to make the king believe what you were saying."

Sergeant Blackwell looked around and shushed Alexei. "You can't just blurt those things out, Lexi."

"Here." Alexei extended his fist towards the Sergeant, to which the Sergeant placed an open palm. Opening his hand, a yellow jewel fell into the Sergeant's palm. "This is one of the jewels that my sisters sewed into my jacket, just a few days before my family was killed. These jewels were the only thing that saved my life that night. If you look at the markings, you'll see imprints of my family's blood. Show this to Cousin George and relay the story. Maybe then he will believe you."

Closing his hand, Sergeant Blackwell looked up at Alexei. "Thank you, your royal highness. I will do what I can and return for you as soon as possible."

Alexei nodded and watched as the Sergeant got back into his car and drove down the long driveway and returned to London.

23

The next morning, Alexei was awoken by a knock on his door. He opened his eyes and rubbed his head, attempting to bring himself back to reality.

"Come in." He uttered in a groggy voice. The door creaked open to reveal Mrs. Swinburn, holding a stack of folded linens in her hand. Her red hair glimmered as the sun beamed in from the window next to the bed.

"Good morning, Lexi." She motioned toward him before making her way in, opening the door fully before entering. She placed the stack of clothes on the dresser near the door. "I hope you don't mind, I brought you some of Eli's old clothes to wear. I'm sure he won't mind you using some of them. I noticed you had nowt when you arrived."

Alexei looked confused for a moment. "Eh...nowt?"

She turned and looked at him, and seemingly started to laugh at herself. "You'll have to excuse me. My northern English accent gets the better of me sometimes." Shaking her head, she picked up one of the white cotton shirts, allowing it to unfold.

"'Nowt' means 'nothing'".

"Ah..." He shook his head slightly, motioning to her that he understood. "So does that mean 'owt' means 'anything'?" he said jokingly, a smile painted across his face.

Mrs. Swinburn grinned. "That's...actually correct." She laughed as Alexei looked taken aback for a moment. "Quite a smart brain you have there." Folding the shirt back onto the stack, she made her way back towards the door. "Everything should fit. Why don't you try a few things on and let me know if anything needs mending." With a nod, she grabbed the door and shut it behind her.

Rising from the bed, Alexei made his way over to try on a few of the clothes. Most of the items looked exceedingly common. Just a few pairs of brown trousers, white shirts, and socks. All seemed to look like it would fit appropriately. Unbuttoning his shirt, he slid it off his arms, revealing the bandage that was still holding from his last cleaning in Nice. Slowly, he peeled the bandage off, the scabbing of the wound had begun to show. This caused Alexei to sigh in relief, completely removing the bandage before throwing on the baggy cotton shirt, followed by a new pair of trousers and his boots.

Making his way downstairs, he noticed Mr. Swinburn in the parlor reading a newspaper. Squinting his eyes, Alexei could make out the top headline. *'Russian Bolshevik's Overtake Revolution. Royal Family Feared Dead.'* The top of the newspaper showed the date, 29th of July 1918.

It had been only a week and a half since his family had been murdered, and the Bolshevik regime was already proclaiming victory as if they had known what was best for the people of Russia. Alexei had studied communism and Karl Marx in his history lessons, a war cry from the working class against capitalism. He had tried to talk to his father regarding his lessons, warning him of things that could happen, but he would not listen. His sisters had even attempted to do the same, only to have the same outcome. Capitalism seemed to be a means to an end, however, he hadn't thought that the end would be so bloody.

"You sleep all right?" He heard Mr. Swinburn's voice bellow from behind the newspaper.

"Yes, sir." Alexei nodded in his direction, even though he couldn't see him.

"Good." Placing the paper down in his lap, he looked over at Alexei. "The girls and Eli are out doing some chores. Why don't you join them?"

Another nod, this time noticeable. "Of course." He turned his feet in the direction of the front door and made his way out, nodding to Mrs. Swinburn in the kitchen on the way, who gently smiled.

The air outside seemed calm. A light breeze blew through the trees, causing the leaves to rustle against one another. The overcast sky above was filled with grey clouds, but he could see the sun barely poking through in the distance.

Taking a deep breath, he looked around for any sign of Lily, Violet, or Eli. At the far end of the barn, he noticed the two girls running around, as if they were playing a game of touch. Alexei smiled before stepping onto the ground as he made his way over towards the barn.

For just a little while, things seemed peaceful. He wondered if he could just remain here forever. He felt like, for the first time in a very long time, he wasn't afraid for his life. No one around knew who he was, and he welcomed the sense of security.

"Aye, new kid!" He heard a voice come from inside the barn. Shifting his gaze, he noticed Eli amongst a herd of sheep. He turned and started walking in his direction. "Looking for some chores to do?"

Alexei grinned as he approached. "I am looking to help in any way that I can."

Eli grinned in return. "Great! You can start by handing me that bucket on the ground there." Looking down, Alexei noticed a small bucket full of pellets. Reaching down, he grabbed ahold of the handle and lifted it in Eli's direction, who grabbed it from his hands. "Thank you, Lexi." For a moment, Eli seemed to survey him, looking him up and down. "It appears we may be twins today."

Alexei noticed that Eli's outfit reflected almost exactly what he had chosen to wear. "Well, one of us must change." He looked at Eli with a serious face before smiling again.

Eli grinned, pouring the bucket of pellets into the trough for the sheep. "Nah, it'll take too long. We'll just suffer through it together." Placing the bucket back on the ground, he climbed over the top of the fence, meeting Alexei on the other side. "How about I show you around? I don't believe you've been given the grand tour." He said as he dusted his trousers off.

"That sounds wonderful." Alexei motioned towards the door. "Please, lead the way."

Walking outside, Eli looked around before pointing to his left. "Well, that's the house where we live. You've seen that." Next, he pointed behind them. "Behind us is the barn that you were just in, which ain't anything special but it's big." Then he pointed directly in front of him. "And that's the road to London, about a twenty-to-thirty-minute drive."

Eli was right about the barn. Despite holding only a few farm animals, the building was larger than the house they lived in. The white-painted wood showcased the sides with a blackened triangular roof covering it all. The building seemed like it had seen a lot of use over the years.

Turning his attention back to Eli, Alexei could tell that he was still pointing towards the road as if frozen in time. "Have you ever been to London?"

Eli began to drop his hand. "Not so much." He shook his head. "No reason to go, really. Father always takes the trips into town, usually by himself. I go every once in a while, when I have a reason, or just to get away for a bit."

"How does your father know Sergeant Blackwell?" Alexei seemed genuinely curious.

Eli squinted. "They served a little time in the war together.

Father was discharged but they remained close. Tommy...er... Sergeant Blackwell comes to visit quite often, in fact. He usually brings Lily and Violet something from his travels. This time...he brought you."

Looking over at Eli he could tell that he was curious as to why the Sergeant would bring him here. "I am grateful for the Sergeant."

"He seems to know the right people." Eli patted Alexei's back. "Don't worry, I'm sure whoever he's trying to get into contact with will get back to him. Then you'll be reunited with your family."

The sentence caused Alexei to cringe. If only Eli had known the truth behind what he just said, he was sure that he would not have phrased it that way. Despite Eli's ignorance, he tried to change the subject. "How old are you, Eli?"

"Just turned sixteen last month. Second of June. What about you?" He peered over at Alexei again.

"Thirteen but will be fourteen in a few weeks." He wasn't ready to give away his exact birthday to someone he had only met yesterday.

Eli smirked. "We will have to have a party if you're still here."

Alexei couldn't imagine having a birthday party anymore. His last birthday was spent locked up in a house in Siberia with his siblings. The one before that he remembered was as lavish as they come. The Royal Palace was always known for throwing extravagant parties, sometimes for no special occasion. His twelfth birthday at the palace had been something to remember. There was music, dancing, and food, and everyone seemed to enjoy themselves. He would always watch as his sisters danced on the floor with their father, taking turns as he would spin them into the arms of another man or back towards their mother, depending on whatever his father had deemed appropriate.

Smiling at the thought, Alexei responded. "Perhaps..."

Suddenly, he felt a thud on the back of his legs, causing

him to turn around and see Lily and Violet standing inside the barn. Looking down, he could see they had kicked a football toward him. "Hey!"

Eli picked up the ball and hurled it back at the girls. "You should give us a warning next time!" Taking a wide stance, he looked back at them as they smiled. "Come on, let's see what you got!"

With that, Violet took a shot, kicking the ball directly at Eli, who quickly blocked it with his left arm. He immediately picked it up and threw it back.

"Is that all you got?" Eli yelled in their direction. Alexei couldn't help but smile. "Come on then!"

Lily gave the ball a kick, which rolled slowly toward Eli's feet. For a moment, Eli didn't move, then as soon as the ball got to his feet, he lunged down and covered the ball with his whole body, causing Lily and Violet to laugh.

"You almost got it, Lily! So close!" He stood up and threw the ball back toward the pair.

Violet caught the ball and placed it under her foot. She looked up. "Lexi! You next!"

Eli looked at Alexei for a sign of approval. "I...I've never played before."

"It's easy!" Eli said, motioning for him to come closer. "You just stand here and wait for them to kick it. Then, you block in the direction you think the ball is going to go."

"A... all right." Stepping into the space where Eli had been, Alexei stood there, waiting for Violet to kick the ball.

"Widen your stance!" Eli said next to him. "Cover more ground area!" He spread his legs to position himself better for the ball.

With a swift kick, Violet sent the ball flying in his direction. Before he knew it, he threw his hands up in front of his face as the ball hit his arms and fell to the ground.

"Violet!" He heard Eli scold her. "You know better than to aim at someone's face!"

"I was just playing, Eli! Yeesh..." Violet scoffed before

stomping off.

Placing his arms down, Alexei could still see the white football in front of him, and an anxious Lily waiting to intercept. He kicked the ball slightly, sending it rolling in her direction.

"That's weak." She said bluntly before catching the ball with her foot. "Ready!?" She shouted at Alexei, to which he nodded. Another kick and the ball rolled in his direction. He felt that this would have been an easy one to catch, but instead decided to let the ball roll, as he slowly motioned towards it before seeing it pass by him. Lily cheered. "I did it!"

Violet scoffed again. "Because he let you win."

Alexei looked back at the girls. "That was a really fast ball, Lily! Where did you get that strength?" Lily and Alexei laughed together.

Eli appeared beside him, the ball now in his hands. "All right, new kid." Passing the ball, he placed it into Alexei's hands. "Time to show me what you've got." He motioned for him to join the girls.

"You want me to kick it?" Alexei asked confusingly.

Eli looked back at him. "Nope, I want you to stand there and hold the ball while we all admire you with it." The girls laughed again but Alexei didn't seem amused by the joke. "Of course, I want you to kick it!"

Walking towards Lily and Violet, Alexei tossed the ball in the air a couple of times before turning around and facing Eli, who was already positioned in a wide stance.

"Come on, new kid. Show me what you got!"

Placing the ball on the ground, Alexei positioned himself in the direction of Eli. Around him, the frame of the barn made up an almost perfect goal. Arching his foot back, he took a deep breath as he kicked the ball forcefully, watching as it made its way towards the other side of the barn.

Before Eli could react, the ball soared past the upper-right corner of the barn door and flew outside. "Hey! That's not fair!" The girls laughed again as they proceeded to run after the ball. "I wasn't ready!"

Alexei laughed. "Uh huh...sure."

Eli shook his head. "Beginner's luck."

For a little while longer, they stayed outside playing football, taking turns shooting at the goal of the barn door. Alexei felt like he hadn't had this much fun in a long time, and, for a moment, his past disappeared. Something as simple as a game of football had caused him to put his other feelings aside and focus on what was in front of him. When the thought finally returned of who he was, there was a moment of shame, feeling as if he had forgotten about his real family.

That afternoon, Mr. Swinburn took Eli out to the fields to assist him in some farming activities. Alexei decided to stay behind with the girls and Mrs. Swinburn, with whom he spent a considerable amount of time cleaning the house, occasionally stopping to play hide and seek with Lily and Violet. Mrs. Swinburn didn't say too much during the day but seemed very grateful for his willingness to help around the house.

The evening felt almost the same as the one before, even though Sergeant Blackwell was not present. Everyone sat in the same seat, the same grace was said, and leftovers were served. Alexei looked around as the family dined on their meals. Eli and Mr. Swinburn returned from the field and were covered in dirt and mud, and their hands were washed immediately upon entering the house.

After dinner, Alexei went upstairs to his room. He promptly lit a candle that was sitting on the dresser. The light illuminated the rest of the room as he looked around. Changing into the night clothes Mrs. Swinburn had neatly laid out for him on his bed, he thought about how well his day had been. He wondered if his family would be angry at him for being so immersed in the Swinburn's, or would they be happy that he might be one step closer to freedom.

Looking in the mirror above the dresser, he remembered gazing at himself while he was in Nice. He felt as if he had grown five years older in just a matter of weeks. His face looked even older since the last time he took a good look at himself. The only thing he felt thankful for was the fact he didn't have any grey hairs, at least not yet. His reddish-brown hair still seemed to maintain its original color.

A knock came from the door as he turned his head.

"Yes?"

As the door opened, he noticed Eli's blond hair poking in, followed by his face, now appearing much cleaner than earlier. "Hey ya. Can I come in?"

Alexei nodded, permitting him to enter. The door swung open as Eli stepped in. "I just wanted to check on you and make sure the rest of your day went okay." Eli looked over at Alexei, who was still standing in front of the mirror. "The girls didn't run ya around too hard, eh?"

Chuckling slightly, Alexei shifted his weight. "Not at all. They are delightful company."

"Who do you think you're foolin'?" Eli laughed. "Nah, they're all right."

"Is this how every day is around here?" Alexei asked, unsure of which answer he would get.

Eli squinted. "You mean chores in the morning, house and farm work in the afternoon, supper in the evening, and bed?" Alexei was baffled at how quickly he rattled that off. "Yep, that about sums it up. Living the marvelous life of Riley."

"Who?" Alexei became confused at Eli's comment.

"Ah, just some expression my father says. Pay it no mind." Eli laughed. "Anyway, I was just making sure you were all right. If you need anything else, just let me know. I'm just one door down! Two, if you're drunk."

Alexei laughed again, this time more vocally. "Thank you, Eli. I will see you in the morning."

With a nod, Eli grabbed the door and closed it behind him.

24

Two weeks passed, and every day was almost exactly as Eli had described it. Waking up, Alexei would join the family for breakfast. Then, he and Eli would venture outside to the barn for the morning chores of taking care of the sheep and cleaning up the barn, followed by Eli getting swept away with his father for farming duties and Alexei would go inside and help with chores. The evening dinners always seemed so nice. The family appeared to enjoy being together during their meals. Some nights, they would all sit in the parlor afterward where Eli and his parents would read stories to Violet and Lily. Afterward, everyone would venture up to bed, and Eli would come in and check on Alexei before going to his room.

This morning felt different though. Opening his eyes, he scrunched his neck down towards his blanket, attempting to shield his face. He knew what day it was. The twelfth of August; his fourteenth birthday. The first year that he would have a birthday without his family present. He laid in bed for a little while longer, knowing that he might miss breakfast if he waited too long. He wondered if someone would come and check on him.

Tears ran down his face as he thought about his sisters. For his last few birthdays in the palace, and before their imprisonment, Anastasia would always wake him up and take him downstairs to the Great Hall where an abundance of food would be waiting for them, as well as his other sisters and mother and father. They would feast in the morning followed by a carriage ride after he was properly dressed. Olga would always see to it that he was able to get into the carriage without getting hurt, and Maria would tease him constantly about it. The ride would go through the countryside and circle back into St. Petersburg. In the evening, they would hold a lavish ball where people flocked in droves to celebrate the birthday of the crown prince. He would often sit on the throne with his mother while his father danced the night away with his sisters. Sometimes Alexei would get ornery and play pranks and tricks on his sisters, to which they would always scold him. He once stole a whole rack of lamb and hid it in Tatiana's chamber. When she found it on the third day, it had already been infested with flies. Alexei remembered how mad she was, and how much his father had admonished him for such a prank.

A laugh escaped him as another tear ran down his cheek. Pulling the blanket away from his face, he decided to get up and get dressed for the day. He pulled on another white shirt, brown trousers, and boots, and threw on his green vest, which he hadn't put on since he arrived. Mrs. Swinburn had seen to it that his clothes were thoroughly washed, including his vest. He thought that today might be special, even if nobody else thought it was, and he would wear the vest as a symbol.

Making his way out of his room, he walked down the stairs to see Mrs. Swinburn walking past the stairwell, her red hair in a bun on top of her head.

"Look at your snazzy outfit!" She said from the kitchen as she looked at him reaching the bottom step. "You going to a party?"

Alexei smiled. "Just wanted to look a little nicer today, that's all."

Mrs. Swinburn pulled a loaf of bread out of the oven. "Well don't go showing all of us up now, you hear? People are liable to think there's money in this house, and the last thing we need's a snoop." She smiled at him in return, then motioned for him to head outside.

Opening the door, Alexei stepped into the daylight. The sun had just risen but he could already feel the heat on his face. Today was going to be a very hot day. He stepped down and made his way over to the barn, where he assumed Eli would be waiting for him.

Upon entering the barn, he noticed that the sheep had already been fed, and Eli was nowhere to be found. Curiously, all the hay that they needed to move for the day had already been done as well. Becoming skeptical, Alexei turned around and walked back to the house, opening the door to go back inside.

"Have you seen Eli?" Alexei asked, as he noticed his accent had begun to dilute over the last two weeks.

Mrs. Swinburn responded from the kitchen. "He left with his father to go run errands. They should be back in a bit." Alexei was just about to leave when he heard her voice speak up once again. "Oh! I almost forgot to tell you. A letter came for you yesterday."

Suddenly, his body went cold. Somebody knew where he was, but who? He tried not to overreact as he made his way to the kitchen, where Mrs. Swinburn was finishing cutting the bread that she had taken out of the oven earlier.

"A letter?"

Dusting off her hands, she reached into her apron pocket and pulled out a sealed envelope. "It's addressed to my husband, but your first name is right next to his. I'm assuming it is from Tommy...er...Sergeant Blackwell." She paused before handing over the letter to him.

With a simple nod, he accepted the letter and turned around to walk towards the parlor, slowly chipping away at the seal on the back. When the adhesive finally gave way, he opened it up to reveal a one-page letter dated the tenth of August 1918.

'Lexi,

I hope your stay with the Swinburn's is going accordingly. Albert and I have been friends for years so I knew that he would see to it that you were properly taken care of. His family has always been dear to me, and I trust them with my life. I hope that you may come to realize that same thing.

I know you have been waiting for my correspondence regarding your meeting with your cousin. Sadly, his advisor has not agreed to a meeting yet. I do ask that you wait a little while longer. We did know that this wasn't going to be easy, but with a little more time, I feel that I can convince the advisor that you are who you say you are. One way or another, I will make sure you get where you need to be.

Please know that I am doing everything in my power to ensure your safety.

Sincerely,
Sergeant Thomas Blackwell'

Folding the letter and placing it back into the envelope, Alexei placed it in his pocket. He wasn't sure exactly how to feel about the situation. On the one hand, speaking to Cousin George was the reason he was in England in the first place. If he were to grant him amnesty, Alexei could see to it that his return to Russia would be simply to restore the throne that was overtaken by the Bolsheviks and return order to his motherland. On the other hand, a life without royal worry these last few weeks had been a bit of a reprieve from his duties as the crown prince. Hard labor was not his strong suit, but he didn't seem to mind the other duties of a simpler life, and he had grown to enjoy the Swinburn family. Taking care of Lily and Violet gave him a sense that he was giving something back for what his sisters had given him. His friendship with Eli had even started to grow, and he knew for sure that that was something he was going to miss when he eventually had to leave.

"Everything all right, dear?" Mrs. Swinburn looked over at him, leaning against the archway from the parlor into the hall.

His face straightened up as he looked back at her. "Yes. Sergeant Blackwell was just giving me an update on his... search."

She seemed to see through his defensive demeanor. "Well, whatever he's looking for, I hope he finds it for you." She smiled and then turned around, heading back into the kitchen.

Alexei sat down in one of the parlor chairs, thinking about what to do next with his morning. To his left, he noticed the morning newspaper sitting on the stand, meaning that Mr. Swinburn must have read it before venturing out with Eli. Picking it up Alexei began to thumb through the articles.

The front page was littered with news of the war, the main story being that a British pilot named Stuart Culley had shot down one of the German's zeppelins. Turning the page, another article dealt with a French troopship getting torpedoed by a German submarine, where nineteen soldiers were killed. Then, at the bottom of the page, he noticed another article that caught his eye.

'Pope Benedict XV Asks Bolshevik Leaders to Allow Ex-Tsarina and Family to Quit Russia'

Alexei shook his head, knowing it was much too late for such a cause. Once his father had abdicated, the Bolsheviks took control and made sure his family would never escape. Of course, the Bolshevik regime would answer a resounding 'no' to this request as they had no family to give in the first place.

He wondered for a moment where those soldiers had taken his family. Out in the middle of nowhere, far away from public view, where no one would find their bodies. Only the soldiers would know where they were, and he didn't figure any of them would ever divulge that kind of information.

Folding the paper back the way it was, he returned it to the stand before rising from the seat and walking over to the parlor door. For some reason, the news of the Pope wanting to evacuate the family made him sick to his stomach. Suddenly, the world seemed to care for the royal family's safety and wanted to harbor them in their country, be they allies or enemies. All for nothing, which he was sure they would figure out soon enough.

Alexei returned upstairs and shut himself in his room for the remainder of the day, trying to keep himself from crying whenever he thought about his family. He clenched his eyes shut and laid in his bed until evening when a knock came from his bedroom door.

Hesitating to respond, he arose from bed, wiping his eyes just in case. He walked over to the door and opened it. Eli stood there, his boots tapping against the hardwood floor.

"Finally!" He said as he waved his hands in front of him. "Everyone's been worried sick about you. Are you all right?"

Alexei opened the door further, then turned around to walk back towards his bed. "I...I will be." He took a moment to compose himself. "I do appreciate you coming to check on me. It's very kind."

"That's what friends do, Lexi." Eli's footsteps could be heard moving closer.

"Friends?" Alexei snapped back. "You barely know me, Eli. How could you consider me a friend so quickly?"

For a moment, there was silence. Then, Alexei felt a hand on his shoulder. "Time is not a requirement for a friendship. Sometimes you just...know when you are going to get on with someone. Old people revel in time and the fact that they couldn't get enough of it before they die. Why would I base my friendships on that?" Alexei turned to face him. "Do you not consider me a friend?"

Alexei had to think for a moment. The term 'friend' had lingered through his mind since he had escaped Yekaterinburg with Luka. He thought of Luka as a friend for helping him escape and get somewhere safe. He considered Reggie as a friend for protecting him when he couldn't protect himself. Thinking further, he struggled to think about what he had given them in return, but couldn't come up with anything, which caused him to clench his fists. These people who he had considered friends had done so much for him, but he must have seemed useless and powerless in their eyes.

He returned focus on the conversation with Eli, whom he realized he might have left hanging on the question a little longer than he expected. He turned around to see Eli slightly hanging his head, his blonde hair falling into his face. He and Eli had spent every day together since he had arrived on the farm, and yet they barely knew anything about each other. Still, Eli always made sure that Alexei was included in every activity and every game that Lily and Violet wanted to play with him.

"I…" Alexei hesitated as Eli lifted his head slightly. "Of course, I do, Eli."

Immediately, a smile appeared on Eli's face. "Great! Because I've got something to show you. Follow me!"

Taken aback, Alexei looked around as if Eli were playing a joke on him. It wasn't until Eli motioned for him at the door that he finally stepped forward in his direction.

"Where are we going?" Alexei seemed confused as they began walking downstairs.

"You'll see." That was all Eli said as they walked. He waved to his parents who were sitting in the parlor, and Alexei waved behind him. They nodded in return.

Eli continued towards the front door and then outside to the barn. Alexei followed close behind, wondering what Eli was doing and why he needed to follow him outside. From the sky, Alexei could tell it was late in the evening as the sun had just begun to set. He wasn't sure how long he had spent in his room, but his surroundings told him that it had been most of the day.

Approaching the barn, Eli turned to face him. "Close your eyes."

Uneasy, Alexei glared momentarily at Eli before fully closing his eyes. He felt a hand wrap around his arm, leading him into the barn. A few steps later, they stopped.

"Stay right there a moment, and don't open your eyes."

Alexei did as he was told. He wasn't sure what Eli was

about to do, but he was almost positive he wasn't in any danger. Clenching his eyelids, he forced himself not to peek. He tried to suspend his curiosity, hearing some loud banging in front of him that almost made him jump. A couple of times he heard Eli grunt, as if he were moving things around in the barn.

"Okay, you can open them." He heard Eli say on the other side of the room. Slowly, he opened his eyes.

Around him, hundreds of fireflies flew, lighting up the inside of the barn. The sight was spectacular, each bug with its own rhythm, some flashing in sync with each other, others flickering to a tune of their own. On the wall, two lanterns were dimly lit to show a banner that simply read 'Happy Birthday, Lexi!'.

"Whoa..." Alexei let out a gasp of amazement. "This is incredible, Eli! How did you catch all these fireflies?"

Eli was proud of himself; his smile stretching from ear to ear. Alexei was sure his smile looked the same. "Believe me, it took a few days, but it was worth it though to see the look on your face."

Alexei couldn't take his eyes off the fireflies around him, blinking flashes of light near his face. "I can't believe you put all this together. Simply beautiful."

Eli approached him, his hands behind his back. "That's not all." He moved his hands from behind him to reveal a small brown satchel. "Here." Reaching out his hand, Alexei grabbed the satchel.

Alexei began untying the strings as he spoke. "But how did you know it was my birthday?"

"You told me." Eli said as Alexei looked up confused. "Well...you told me it was in a few weeks and so I just decided that, if I wasn't going to get a date out of you, I would just give you a little party anyways." Alexei's grin got wider, causing Eli to cock his head. "Wait, is today your actual birthday?"

Alexei smiled. "It is."

"Well, lucky me! I suppose I'm just a good guesser." Eli seemed amazed at himself.

Finishing untying the strings on his satchel, Alexei could feel a long strand of something from the outside of it. Tipping it over into his hands, he noticed a leather rope necklace fall out with a charm on it. Looking closer, he could have sworn he had seen the charm before. Then it hit him. The item that was attached to the necklace was a silver ruble, a coin from his motherland. The ruble had a man looking to the left. It was the face of the previous Tsar of Russia, Alexei's father, Nicholas.

Tears formed in his eyes and began to trickle down his cheek. He hadn't seen his father's face in quite some time, and this was a very unexpected gift. Tears continued pouring down his face, and there was nothing he could do to stop them. He took his hand and wiped both sides of his cheeks before looking back up at Eli, who appeared stunned.

"I...uh...didn't think a coin on a necklace would cause you to cry so much." Eli shifted his stance. "Is it...bad?"

Alexei shook his head. "Absolutely not!"

"When we first met, I noticed your accent. I thought this might remind you a little bit of home." Eli shifted again, looking for a sign of approval from Alexei.

Looking up at him, Alexei smiled. "It's perfect, Eli."

Biting his lower lip, Eli examined Alexei's face. "I've never seen anyone cry so much over a coin though."

"Eli..." Alexei began as he wiped more tears from his eyes. "This man...on the coin...it's..."

"Tsar Nicholas II. I know." Eli seemed impressed with himself. "It's a bloody shame what they did to him. His family must be a wreck."

For a moment, Alexei thought about what to say next. He wasn't sure if giving away his secret was a good idea, even if Eli had been so kind to him. Smiling, he took the necklace and placed it over his head, allowing the coin to fall onto his chest as the leather rope wrapped around his neck. "Thank you for this. I wish I had something to give you in return."

"Don't mention it." Eli placed his hand on Alexei's shoulder, rocking him back and forth slightly in a playful manner. “Happy Birthday, Lexi.”

They both smiled.

25

A few more days passed, and Eli and Alexei became even closer. In the mornings, Alexei would help with the chores as he usually did. In the afternoons, he started joining Mr. Swinburn and Eli in the fields once the dew had run off all the plants. They harvested beetroot and lettuce, picking everything that looked ready to harvest and filling up large sacks that they carried around with them. Then they would return them to the house where Mrs. Swinburn, along with Lily and Violet, would clean and prepare them.

The evenings were spent in the same manner, eating dinner, and then sitting in the parlor for reading or conversation. Eli would often tinker with some gadget, then pass it over to Alexei to do the same. Mr. Swinburn would finish reading the paper, then ask Alexei if he would like to read it, which he had usually already skimmed through earlier in the day, looking for news from back home. The last few days had been surprisingly uneventful with news of his family or the Russian resistance. He wasn't sure if that was a good thing, but he tried not to think about it too much. Instead, he enjoyed his time with the family he had in front of him. Over the last couple of weeks, they had taken care of him and made sure he was clothed and fed. He couldn't have been more grateful.

The next morning, Mrs. Swinburn asked if Alexei could help with keeping the girls busy while she ran an errand in town. Mr. Swinburn was already out in the fields with Eli and the errand wouldn't take more than a couple of hours. Alexei agreed to watch Lily and Violet while she was out.

Walking them outside, Lily immediately ran over to the barn, shouting at her sister. "Come on! Let's play tag!"

Violet followed, motioning for Alexei to join them. "We should follow before she hurts herself."

Running into the barn, Lily had already found a hiding spot near the sheep, although she was clearly visible as she poked her head out to check.

"Wait!" Alexei said as Violet turned toward him. "Who is 'it'?"

Violet smiled as she tagged his shoulder. "You are!" She ran in the opposite direction towards the other side of the barn, and Alexei chased her.

Jumping over the fence into the sheep pen, Violet headed toward Lily, who was still hiding behind a trough. Alexei made his way over to the fence and began opening the gate.

Lily shouted. "He's got us trapped!" She hunkered down even further behind the trough.

"Speak for yourself!" Violet shouted as she made her way back to the gate, leaping just as she did to get in and making her way for the barn door.

Alexei stood there for a moment, deciding whether to chase Violet or tag Lily, as she seemed to be the easy target. Turning around, he closed the gate again and made his way for the barn door.

"Hey!" He heard Lily shout from behind him. Alexei didn't bother to turn around. Instead, he made his way toward the opening of the barn, watching as Violet ran back towards the house.

Planting his feet on the ground, he darted for her, attempting to make long strides. The last time he had run so fast was when he was escaping the soldiers almost a month ago, in the pouring rain. He thought about that for a moment before returning to reality, where Violet was waiting for him at the front door of the house.

"Aren't you going to run?" Alexei asked as he approached.

Violet smiled. "Quick, tag me." She held out her hand.

"What? Why?" He was confused, reaching out his hand to touch hers.

Her smile grew wider. "You'll see." Their hands touched as she flew past him back towards the barn where Lily was exiting. Running up to her, Alexei followed a few steps behind. "Lily! You've got to watch out!"

"He's coming!" Lily yelled as she retreated into the barn again. "Violet, hurry up!"

Violet gained on Lily and brushed her shoulder with her hand. "You're it!"

Lily turned around, astonished by the betrayal. "What!? No fair! That's no fair!"

Turning and running back towards Alexei, Violet looked at him. "You'd better book. She's a fast runner for a small fry."

Alexei turned and made his way back towards the house, Violet running towards the other side. He couldn't tell if Lily had followed him, but he kept running, hoping that he'd made the right decision.

Around the back of the house, the fields were vast, and he could see Eli and Mr. Swinburn off in the distance. He wondered how long they were going to be out there. Spending time with Eli was one of his favorite parts of the day. He had become a great friend, and he was grateful to have someone who cared about him.

Suddenly, Alexei felt his foot get caught on something. A rock about the size of a football was nestled into the ground, causing him to lose his footing. Trying to break his fall, he placed his hands outwards to catch himself. In an instant, he was on the ground, and he felt a sharp pain hit his knee.

"Lexi!" He heard Violet yell from the other end of the house. She rushed over to him, Lily not too far behind her. "Are you all right?"

Taking a deep breath, he turned over to sit on the ground, noticing a small gash on his knee. The wound had already started to pool blood. "Yes, but I think I'll need to get inside quickly." As he tried to stand on his own, Violet suddenly appeared and placed her arm around him, helping prop up his bad knee.

"Lily, go get Daddy and Eli. Tell them that Lexi is hurt." She motioned out towards the field.

Lily sighed. "Does this mean tag is over?"

Turning a side-eye towards her sister, she yelled. "Go!"

Getting back into the house, Violet helped Alexei as he sat down on one of the chairs in the parlor. Moving a small stool over, she placed it in front of the chair. "Put that leg up. I'll find a bandage."

For a moment, he was alone. Looking at his knee, the blood had already run down his leg, covering the majority of it. Blood began making its way toward the back part of his knee. He looked around for something to soak it up but couldn't find anything.

Violet appeared again, this time with a couple of damp cloths in her hand. She first quickly wrapped his knee, attempting to halt the flow of blood. Then she began wiping off blood from his leg.

Alexei shook his head. "You really don't have to do all of that."

With a grin, Violet kept wiping. "Shush."

"Lexi!" He heard Eli shout from the front door as it swung open.

"He's in here!" Violet shouted as she continued her task.

Running into the room, Eli and Mr. Swinburn immediately noticed the blood on Alexei's leg.

Mr. Swinburn moved quickly into the parlor, taking the cloth from Violet, and waving her out of the way. "We need to get a doctor here." He began wiping up blood from Alexei's leg. "Eli, run over to the Carter's. They have a telephone you can use to ring the doctor." Eli nodded and was immediately out the door.

A few moments of clarity came when Alexei noticed the blood seeping through the bandage on his knee.

Mr. Swinburn observed the bandage. "How deep was this cut?"

Before Alexei could respond, he began feeling lightheaded. A few seconds later, Alexei's vision narrowed, and he blacked out.

When he opened his eyes again, he was lying in his bed upstairs. He was surrounded by Mr. and Mrs. Swinburn, as well as another man he had never seen before, who was feeling his head and observing his knee. Looking down, he could see the bandage had been changed and was neatly wrapped.

"I've never seen this kind of thing among common people." The doctor stated his raspy voice, causing Alexei's ears to rise.

Mr. Swinburn looked at the doctor with a concerned face. "What do you mean?"

The doctor shook his head, trying to make sense of what he was observing. "This much bleeding should not have happened with such a small cut. This can only be a sign of hemophilia."

Putting her hand on Alexei's head, Mrs. Swinburn asked, "What is hemophilia?"

"A bleeding disorder..." The doctor stated, rechecking the bandage on Alexei's knee. "...where the blood has a hard time clotting, thus all the bleeding. It's fairly common among members of the royal family, though none are sure of the reason."

The 'royal curse' never had a real name for Alexei, until the doctor spoke the word aloud. He remembered the number of times he had been bedridden early in his childhood, often by a simple cut or a scrape. Every time it happened his mother would fear for his life. There was one time when the pain was so intense, that he wished it would end and prayed for death, but recovery eventually came.

"The disease usually subsides by adulthood, but a lot of them don't even live to see adulthood." Alexei had heard about this before. Many royals born with the curse don't make it past their teenage years, and he wondered if he would suffer the same fate.

Suddenly, he heard Eli's voice echo from the corner of the room. "What can be done?"

Packing up his gear, the doctor looked over at him and said, "Just keep him comfortable. Time is the only thing that can heal this type of illness, unfortunately. Keep him hydrated and don't let him move around too much. In a matter of days, he should be feeling better. This was a minor incident; it could have been much worse."

"Thank you, doctor." Mrs. Swinburn said, nodding in his direction.

Mr. Swinburn opened the door to the bedroom. "I'll show you out."

With that, Mr. Swinburn and the doctor were gone. Mrs. Swinburn stood up and looked over at her son. "Eli, you should let him rest, dear. You haven't even eaten this evening."

Eli looked at her. "I will." He shook his head as if coming out of a trance. "I'll be down shortly."

Mrs. Swinburn walked over to him and hugged him, then looked over at Alexei as she made her way to the door. "Let me know if you need anything." She closed the door behind her, leaving only the two boys in the room.

Standing up, Eli made his way over to the bed. "Did you know?"

Alexei looked at him, obviously knowing what Eli was asking. "I've known ever since I was very young." He shrugged his shoulders. "Doesn't mean that it has stopped me from being a little childish sometimes, it seems."

Shaking his head, Eli looked towards the window. "I know it was only a knee scrape, but once I saw the blood, I got scared." He heard Eli begin to choke on his words. "I was really worried about you, Lexi."

Alexei moved his hand towards Eli. "I appreciate the concern, but you should not worry about me that much. I will be fine." He said, trying to maintain his composure.

Eli shook his head again. "Well, at least now you can't run away when I ask you questions." They both chuckled at the remark.

"I suppose not." Alexei adjusted himself in the bed, trying not to move his leg.

"For now, though, you need to rest. There will be plenty of time to berate you tomorrow." Eli smiled and turned around, making his way toward the door. Before exiting, he turned around to look at Alexei. "Feel better, my friend." With that, he left the room, closing the door behind him.

Alexei shuffled again in bed, trying his hardest to move his leg as little as possible. The bandage was wrapped tightly to secure the wound, as well as a couple of sutures the doctor had put in to close the wound. In his mind, he hoped this bedridden journey would not last as long as others, which tended to last for weeks and sometimes months.

Nestling himself into the blanket, he watched as the candle burned on the dresser on the other side of the room. He knew Mrs. Swinburn would see to it that the candle was put out before retiring for the evening, as she did every night with Violet and Lily.

Looking up at the ceiling, Alexei thought about his situation. Earlier, he had thought about how lucky he was to stay with a family who cared about him. Now, he was even more grateful. It had been ages since he had lived a life of luxury, and living with the Swinburn's was the closest he had come in a year or so, and he wasn't sure that he needed anything more at that moment.

As he closed his eyes, he grasped the necklace around his

neck, holding the ruble with his father's face tightly as he slowly drifted off to sleep.

26

For the next few days, Alexei remained in bed, getting up only when he absolutely needed to. Mrs. Swinburn would check on him every morning and bring him something to eat. Mr. Swinburn would bring the newspaper upstairs after he finished reading it and leave it by the bed. Lily and Violet mainly stayed out of the room, except for the occasional head poke to say hello and ask him how he was doing.

Then there was Eli. In the mornings he would complete his chores and help his father in the fields, before spending every afternoon and evening with Alexei. They would sit together as Alexei read the newspaper, updating Eli of any important events. They mostly talked about the end of the war being in sight and how Germany had very little manpower left to fight. Eli didn't know much about what was going on outside of Great Britain, so he was fascinated learning about the submarines and warships.

After reading the paper, Eli would bring in some cards or a simple game to teach Alexei how to play. Alexei hadn't played a lot of cards when he was in Russia, so Eli took the opportunity to teach him Blackjack. They would spend hours just flipping cards and making imaginary bids. Alexei enjoyed watching Eli laugh as they randomly bid on things such as the dresser, the grass, or the moon.

In the evening, the family would bring their plates upstairs and join Alexei for dinner in his bedroom. They all sat around the bed and chatted about the day, and about what tomorrow would bring. Afterward, everyone would take their dishes downstairs, leaving Alexei a moment of peace to collect his thoughts from the day. Eli would then come back upstairs to spend more time with him.

One evening, Eli asked Alexei about Russia and what it was like. He attempted to describe it in a way that made sense, talking about the mounds of snow during the winter, and the mild temperatures in the summer. His favorite part was talking about the greenery that surrounded all the cities. Someone could get lost for days just traveling from one town to the next.

Another evening, Eli was curious if Alexei had been anywhere besides Russia and Great Britain. Alexei talked about his recent experience in the south of France, describing the city of Nice with as much detail as he could remember. Hearing about Nice's gorgeous architecture and the beaches along the Mediterranean made Eli envious, clearly expressing an interest in wanting to see it for himself one day.

The following night, Eli sat next to Alexei and looked at him with an almost sorrowful demeanor. By this point, Alexei's knee was looking much better, he even thought he might be able to get up and walk around soon, but Eli's face concerned him.

"What's wrong?" Alexei asked hesitantly.

Turning his face away slightly, Eli flinched before responding. "You said you've known about your hema…hemo… whatever it's called, for a long time."

Alexei nodded his head in affirmation. "I have, ever since I was very young."

"Has anyone ever tried to do anything to cure it? Surely there must be something someone can do." Eli shifted again on the bed.

Taking a deep breath, Alexei stared at him. “There...was someone, at one time.” Eli continued staring at him. “He was introduced to our family by my mother. The man proclaimed that he could provide great miracles for those who were worthy of receiving his gift. My mother brought him into our family after one of my...accidents. The man stayed by my side for days, praying and giving me natural medicines that he had procured.”

“Did it work?” Eli asked, squinting his eyes.

“I believe so. I felt better at least. The man read me stories, stayed by my side, and prayed for healing. Honestly, I think having the company was the biggest part of that, and the man was a known healer throughout Russia and Siberia. People loved him and hated him for that.” Alexei hung his head.

“Where is he now? Do you think you could write him? He might have some advice for you.” Shifting again, Alexei heard Eli’s back crack.

“He...is dead. Shot by Russian soldiers a couple of years ago.” Alexei hung his head.

Eli stared at him again, this time his face seemed contemplative. “Wait. This great healer that you knew was killed a couple of years ago. Are you referring to Grigori Rasputin?”

Alexei looked up. “I am.”

“That man was a healer for the Tsar and his family. I heard Father talking about it when they killed him.” Suddenly, Eli looked shocked. “If he was your healer...then that means...Lexi, you’re...”

“Alexei Nikolaevich, Tsarevich of Russia, yes. That is me.” Alexei straightened his posture.

“Shit...” A flabbergasted Eli said, while looking at Alexei as if he were staring at a ghost. “All this time, I’ve been talking to a prince.” He stood up and immediately began to bow.

Alexei threw his hand up. “Eli don’t do that. I expect you to treat me no differently than when we first met. The respect I’ve earned from your family over the last few weeks is greater than the respect demanded from a position of royalty.”

Eli still appeared awestruck. "I...it's just hard to imagine having a prince in this house." He peered out the window again, before asking, "Wait...if you're here...where is your family?"

Alexei closed his eyes. He knew the question would come up eventually, but he still was never ready to speak the words aloud. "They...are gone. All of them."

Sitting back down beside Alexei, Eli placed his hand on his shoulder to comfort him. "I'm sorry, Lexi. I didn't know."

"How could you?" Alexei shrugged. "The Bolshevik regime hasn't had the bravery to announce that anyone, besides my father, was disposed of. The cowards." His face turned red as anger rushed through him.

For a few moments, there was silence.

"Would you tell me about them?" Eli asked as Alexei looked up at him. "Your family. What were they like?"

Alexei was taken aback by the question. Since he had escaped, no one had asked about his family, though it may not have been that they hadn't cared to ask. He looked at Eli's genuinely curious expression, and somehow he felt grateful.

"My family...they were wonderful." He started his explanation, already beginning to tear up. "My father, Nicholas, was a strong man. He had always cared about the future of his country and its people, taking extreme care to ensure its proper place in the world. Sometimes he would visit the military camps, and I would get to join him and watch as he gave inspirational speeches to the soldiers. Hearing the soldiers rally and cheer after his speeches gave me so much hope for the motherland. I suppose that hope has dwindled now." Alexei took a deep breath before continuing. "My mother, Alexandra, stood opposite of father, both in station and in demeanor. Where my father was stern, my mother was kind and caring. Where he saw doubt, she saw clarity. The two opposites made well for parents, especially to someone such as me, an onery boy who liked to get himself into trouble. She always looked out for me and protected me, even when I wasn't deserving of it."

"They sound like quite the pair." Eli interjected, slightly

grinning at his words.

"They were." Alexei nodded. "My sisters, on the other hand, each had a personality all their own. Olga was my eldest sister. She followed mother and father around every chance she could, so I didn't see her as much. She was always the sterner one of my sisters, but I always knew she cared for me. During one of my first accidents, she stayed by my side and kept a thorough journal on my condition, seeing that I was improving with every day that passed." He closed his eyes to imagine her for a moment before continuing.

"Tatiana was next. I always called her 'mother incarnate'. She was the spitting image of mother, and her demeanor and character were also a reflection of her. Even if she didn't follow in mother's footsteps directly, her charisma shined through in her personality."

"Maria was similar, yet somehow different in her own right. She didn't like being around the family as much as the others. Father even accused her of having an affair with a soldier outside of the palace walls. Of course, she denied it, but even I was skeptical if she was seeing someone." Alexei closed his eyes again, this time envisioning his youngest sister.

"Then there was Anastasia. My protector. My guardian angel. The one who would go to the ends of the earth just to ensure my safety. We were inseparable. Every time our parents would fight, she would take me to the music room and play the piano and sing to me. Sometimes I would even sing along."

"It sounds like you really miss them." Eli began tearing up, but he quickly wiped them away.

"I do." Alexei said, as a tear began falling from his eye. "Sometimes I forget that they're gone, but then I remember that I was there. I heard the gunshots. I saw their bodies. I ran away, leaving them behind in that truck to be disposed of."

"How did you survive?" Glancing at the door, Eli quickly looked back in Alexei's direction.

Alexei took a moment to observe his surroundings, checking each side of the bed to find his satchel. When he finally noticed it on the floor, he twisted his body to grab it, but Eli was already in motion and handed it to him. "Thank you." He stated as he opened the strings on the top, loosening the grip and reaching his hand inside, feeling around for the small satchel. Once he had a hold of it, he pulled it out and placed it on the bed. "When we were held captive in Siberia, my sisters started sewing jewels into my clothes, as well as their own."

He tipped over the satchel and let a couple of jewels fall out. "These jewels protected me. They kept me safe from an otherwise impossible situation. The firing squad surely would have made quick work of me, if the pain from the blow didn't cause me to black out."

"Wow..." Eli couldn't seem to find the words to say. "I... didn't know that you'd been through so much, Lexi. Thank you for telling me."

"I trust you, Eli." Alexei fiddled with the jewels in front of him. "Ever since I've been here, you've shown me nothing but kindness. You've treated me like a brother, and I am grateful to you." Grabbing the green jewel in front of him, he handed it to Eli, who seemed reluctant to take it. "I want you to have this, as proof of my faith in our friendship."

Eli shook his head. "I can't take that. Do you know how much that one jewel is worth?"

"Worth enough to get you and your family somewhere safe and new, should it ever be needed. But for now, it's a token of my gratitude and a reminder of my commitment to return the favor." Once again, he extended his hand. Eli turned his hand over and opened his palm as Alexei placed the oval green jewel firmly into his hand. "These jewels have become a symbol, given to those that I trust with my life. Those who have guided me to safe havens, who have ensured my safety by putting their own lives at risk. Anyone I offer it to is deserving and will one day have the favor of their assistance returned to them."

Smiling, Eli clutched the jewel in his hand. "Thank you, Lexi. This means the world to me."

Alexei nodded. "As you and your family mean the world to

me.”

27

For some reason, Alexei could barely sleep. Thoughts of his family rushed through his mind, causing him to toss and turn throughout the night. Talking about them with Eli made them feel somewhat real again but knowing he would never get the chance to see them again caused tears to stream down his face. The sadness never seemed to fade, and he began to wonder if it would ever go away.

The next morning, he opened his eyes after only sleeping a few hours and checked the wound on his knee. Lifting off the bandage, he could see the cut had fully scabbed over. He breathed a sigh of relief before placing the bandage back on and turning himself out of the bed, placing his feet on the hardwood floor, and pushing himself into a standing position. After almost a week of resting, he finally felt like he could get back to helping around the farm.

Getting dressed, Alexei made his way toward the bedroom door and opened it slowly, peering out to see if anyone was in the hall. Once he saw it was clear, he proceeded to slowly walk toward the stairs. His body slightly limped as he grabbed onto the railing, taking the first step on the wooden staircase.

The face of Mrs. Swinburn appeared at the bottom of the stairs; her expression seemed worried. "Lexi, are you sure you should be up yet? The doctor said you need to take time to heal."

Alexei made his way down the stairs slowly. "I'm feeling much better today, Mrs. Swinburn. Thank you for taking the time to look after me while I was down. It really means a lot." He smiled as he made it to the last step.

Drying her hands with her apron, she smiled back at him. "As long as you're feeling better, and you think you can manage, I will leave your abilities up to you. Though, I wouldn't suggest pushing yourself to chores yet."

"Well, that is one way to get out of doing them, I suppose." Alexei said, watching as Mrs. Swinburn's head shook and another smirk appeared on her face.

"Go on then. I'll see to it that you get something to eat shortly." Turning back around and heading into the kitchen, Mrs. Swinburn motioned him towards the front door. He stood there for a moment, contemplating whether it was safe for him to go outside in his condition.

Finally, he made his way towards the door, opening it with ease to reveal the breeze blowing in from outside. Closing his eyes, he let the air hit his cheeks before stepping out and shutting the door behind him.

He knew Eli would most likely be in the barn around this time, and he didn't see any sign of Violet and Lily, which led him to assume they were behind the house. Stepping off the small steps onto the ground, Alexei began his short journey toward the barn. From a distance he could hear the sheep being shuffled around in their pen. As he approached, he noticed Eli in his white shirt and brown trousers, throwing bales of hay into the pen, being careful not to hit any of the sheep. Turning around, Eli noticed Alexei entering the barn.

"Hiya! You're up!" Eli said, seemingly excited to see him. "Feeling better this morning?"

Shaking his head, Alexei smiled. “Much better. The wound is fully scabbed over so I figured it would be safe for me to venture out.”

Grabbing a bucket, Eli moved it in his direction, acting as if he wanted Alexei to take it. “Well then, I guess we’ll put you to work.”

Hesitating, Alexei began to grab for the bucket before Eli yanked it away quickly.

“I’m just taking the piss, Lexi. No work for you today!” He laughed, placing the bucket back down as Alexei breathed a sigh of relief. “You didn’t think I was going to make you work, did you?”

“I wasn’t sure.” Alexei scratched the back of his head as he smiled at him. The two looked at each other for a moment before Eli turned around to grab more hay. “Eli...” Alexei began nervously. “About last night... I know I told you a lot of things about my family and where I come from. I hope that you...”

“You don’t have to tell me, Lexi. I’m not going to say anything to anyone about it. It’s not my place to tell people who you are.” Eli’s face showed that he was telling the truth. Alexei nodded, then turned to look at the sheep. They all seemed to line up along the fence where he was standing, as if waiting for attention. “It looks like they missed you.” Eli grinned as he threw another stack of hay into the pen.

Reaching his hand over the fence, Alexei patted the head of one of the sheep. It reminded him of how Luka and Klara’s dog, Shep, had responded when they first met. The memory caused him to smile again.

Violet appeared in the doorway, her sun-colored dress beaming in the morning light. Her face appeared awestruck when she noticed Alexei standing there.

“Lexi!” He heard Lily shout from behind Violet. She came running up quickly, looking almost identical to her sister in her yellow dress. “You’re up! That means we can play again!”

Violet scolded her with a look. “Lily, Lexi will not be doing any playing right now. He must get fully better first.” She looked up and smiled at him. "But that's not what I came here to tell you."

"What is it, Vi?" Eli asked as he threw another stack of hay into the pen.

"There's some man walking up the drive." Violet pointed in the direction of the driveway, which extended out to the main road. "I don't think I know him."

Eli moved away from the pen and made his way toward the barn door while Alexei remained in his spot next to the fence. Putting his hand on his forehead, he tried to shield the rising sun from his eyes.

"I don't know him either, I don't believe." He said as he turned toward Alexei. "You'd better hide somewhere for now, just in case."

With that, Alexei looked around for a place to hide. On the other side of the barn sat a couple of wooden crates. He decided to take his chances and walked steadily over to them, crouching down enough so he could still peer over and listen if he needed to.

For a few moments, the silence seemed deafening. He wondered who the mystery person would be randomly coming down the drive. If it was Sergeant Blackwell, surely he'd bring a car. Anyone else might be out to cause trouble, and he knew he wasn't in a good enough state to run very far. Still, Alexei sat with his back to the crate, waiting for the mystery person to approach Eli and his sisters.

"Hi there!" He heard Eli shout as if the person was still quite a distance away. "What can we do for you?"

Another moment of silence before he heard a man's voice. "I beg your pardon..." Alexei had heard that voice before. "I was wondering if you would happen to know...well you see, I'm looking for someone."

Peering around the corner, Alexei could barely make out the figure of a young man in a French-cut jacket and vest. His trousers matched his jacket with some very nice leather boots. Alexei stood up from behind the crate in clear view of the man.

"Reggie?"

Reggie looked at Alexei, who seemed stunned to see him. "Lexi!" He made his way through the three siblings and into the barn. The two men embraced in a brief hug. "I'm so glad that I found you!"

"It's good to see you, Reggie." Alexei began to tear up, except this time for a good reason. "I can't believe you're here! How did you find me?"

Reggie took a deep breath, squaring Alexei up and down for a moment. "LeBlanc had intel from Blackwell of possible places where you might be. He sent me to find you and make sure you were safe."

"LeBlanc is alive?" Alexei interrupted.

"Indeed. He'll be down for a while though. That gunshot left him without the use of his right arm." Taking another deep breath, Reggie seemed to grin at the sight of Alexei.

Eli shook his head, unaware of what was taking place in front of him. "Would someone mind telling me what's going on?"

Both looked in Eli's direction. Violet and Lily stood beside him, just as flabbergasted as he was. Alexei motioned his eyes at the girls and Eli motioned for them to leave, shooing them in the direction of the house. Hanging their heads, the sisters complied.

Alexei approached Eli, Reggie in tow. "Eli, this is Aspirant Reginald Bellion III." Reggie seemed to flinch at the formal title. "Reggie aided me when I was in France. His Uncle Luka brought me there from Russia so that I would be safe."

Reggie put out his hand to shake Eli's. Squinting in suspicion, Eli grabbed his hand and shook it, causing Reggie to grin. "Well, any friend of Lexi's is a friend of mine, I suppose."

"Don't worry, I would be wary also. You have nothing to fear from me, I can assure you." Turning back towards Alexei, Reggie continued. "Lexi, I need to speak with you regarding your stay here." He looked over at Eli, giving a hint that he wanted to be alone. "But..."

"You do not have to worry about Eli. I've told him the truth. He is the only one who knows though." Alexei looked at Reggie's face, expressing concern that Alexei had revealed his true identity.

For a moment, Reggie stood there not saying anything, just looking back at the two of them. "Fine. It's about your journey to see the king."

"The king?" Eli interrupted. "As in King George? You're going to meet with the king!?"

"That is the plan. I have entrusted Sergeant Blackwell with the task of seeing that it happens." Alexei looked over at Eli, watching as he shook his head in disbelief.

"That is what I wanted to discuss, your royal highness... er...Lexi." Reggie tried to pull Alexei's focus back on him. "LeBlanc got some intel that there may be something amiss with this upcoming meeting. Have you heard from Blackwell about any success?"

Alexei sighed. "No. The only letter I received was a week or so ago saying that he had not secured a meeting."

"So, it has been a while since you have heard from Blackwell then?" Reggie seemed to push for an answer.

Alexei nodded. "Not since the letter." He squinted. "Why?"

Reggie looked over at Eli again, who had now gotten closer to the pair. "I have reason to believe that your presence in Great Britain has been relayed to the Bolshevik regime."

"By whom?" Alexei asked, seemingly concerned again as he felt the sweat begin to bead on his forehead.

"I am not sure. LeBlanc got the intel from a peer as a rumor. That is why he sent me to find you. He wants me to move you to another location until a meeting can be secured." Reggie looked over at Eli, who seemed to be taking the whole thing in.

"What about the Sergeant?" Alexei wondered aloud.

Reggie looked back at him. "I will inform him of your new whereabouts as soon as we get there. There is a safehouse in downtown London. We should be secure there until a meeting with the king can be granted, but we must leave as soon as you are ready."

Shifting his leg, Alexei felt a twinge of pain shoot through his knee. "Does it have to be today?" He rolled up his pant leg to expose his bandage. "I had a bit of a fall, you see. Took some time to recover."

Reggie stared at the wound for a moment, contemplating his next thought. "You need to be able to escape if necessary." He sighed. "Yes, we will wait until tomorrow." He turned to Eli, who seemed a bit sad. "Eli, would you mind asking if another friend could stay the night?" Reggie looked at his surroundings. "I could sleep in the barn if it suits you."

Eli rolled his eyes. "As much amusement as that would be, I'm sure we can find a place for you inside." He turned his attention to Alexei and nodded before turning around and heading towards the house.

"I can't believe you survived Paris, Reggie. I thought you were dead." Alexei seemed to be letting his emotions show as another tear fell from his eye. "You and your family have fought hard to keep me safe. I am grateful."

"That is what we do, Lexi. We protect each other." Reggie's words reflected what Eli had said the night before.

"Come on. Let's get inside. I'm sure Mrs. Swinburn will want to know if there's another mouth to feed." Alexei led the way toward the house.

After getting permission for Reggie to stay at the residence, Reggie joined Alexei and the Swinburn family for breakfast, talking about his journey from France and his search to find his long-lost friend, Alexei. In the afternoon, Reggie joined Eli and Mr. Swinburn out in the field gathering crops while Alexei attempted to do some light house chores with the assistance of Violet and Lily, who kept asking him if he was alright. During dinner, the family gathered around the table, and Alexei announced he would be leaving in the morning with Reggie for London.

Mr. Swinburn did not seem very pleased with the news. "I believe that the order was for Thomas...er...Sergeant Blackwell to come and retrieve you when the time was right."

Reggie took a drink of water before interjecting. "That's correct, Mr. Swinburn. Sergeant Blackwell will be notified of his new location. There has just been a slight change of plans due to some new information that has come to light."

Mrs. Swinburn seemed sad at the thought of Alexei leaving. "Well, you've only been here a few weeks, but you've grown on us all quite a bit." She smiled. "I know you have to do what's best for you."

"So why don't you stay?" Eli interrupted, seemingly upset. "Don't go with Reggie. Don't go with Blackwell. Just stay here." His comment was met with a resounding 'yeah' from both Lily and Violet. "You're basically family, Lexi. I don't understand why you can't just stay here."

Alexei looked down for a moment. "I'm sorry, Eli. This is something that I must do. I do not have a choice."

"I do not believe that." Eli said as he shook his head, looking down at his plate.

Mr. Swinburn interrupted. "That will be enough. If Lexi says that he needs to go, we must respect his decision."

The rest of the dinner was mostly silent.

Afterward, Alexei led Reggie upstairs to his bedroom, where Mrs. Swinburn had laid out an extra set of blankets on the floor for Reggie to sleep on. Suggesting that they go to bed early, Reggie excused himself to go change.

A few moments later, Alexei heard a knock on the door. "Come in." He said as Eli poked his head in, allowing the door to open as he entered.

"Am I interrupting anything?" Eli asked, his face still sour looking from dinner.

"Not at all." Alexei said, motioning for him to come closer. Sitting on the bed, he patted the spot beside him, allowing Eli to sit down. "I'm sorry that all of this happened so fast, Eli. I wish there was something I could do to make this better."

Eli shook his head. "It's okay, Lexi. I'm sorry for my comments earlier. You and I have gotten very close over the last few weeks, and I feel like I can tell you anything. It is an awful feeling to just have that ripped from you suddenly."

Alexei placed his hand on Eli's back. "I understand. In any other case, I wouldn't want to leave." He watched as a tear slid down Eli's cheek. "This may be my only chance to meet with Cousin George, and Reggie is trying to make sure that it happens. I don't know what the outcome will be. Who knows, I may even end up back here. You may just be stuck with me forever." He grinned as Eli did the same. "But for now, I must do this. Please understand that."

"I understand, Lexi." Eli looked over at the set of blankets on the floor. "Reggie will see you safely there. He seems like the type of person who wouldn't let you down."

Alexei smiled at him. "And neither would you, Eli." The comment caused Eli to grin as they looked at each other for a moment.

Standing back up, Eli stretched his arms into the air. "I'd better let you get some rest. You have a very busy day tomorrow." He walked over to the door before turning around again and saying, "Goodnight, your royal highness."

28

When Alexei woke up the next morning, he felt as if he'd been asleep for days. Letting out a yawn, he put his arms in the air to stretch. He figured having Reggie in the room made him feel safer than he had in a very long time, which is what contributed to the quality of his sleep.

Looking over his shoulder, he noticed Reggie was still fast asleep on the floor, and he wondered what time it was. Looking out of the window, he could see the sun was just starting to rise, signifying that it was probably close to six in the morning.

Placing his feet carefully on the floor, Alexei maneuvered around slowly so he didn't wake Reggie. Slipping on his white button-down shirt, green vest, and brown trousers, he made his way towards the door, and he noticed that Reggie had hung his jacket on the doorknob. Cautiously grabbing for the jacket, he placed it on top the dresser before turning the handle.

The door creaked, causing Reggie to stir, but not fully wake up, only turning over and then continuing to sleep. Closing the door slowly, he heard more rustling from inside his room.

"You're just going to leave me in here?" He heard Reggie say in a tired voice. Alexei opened the door to see him now sitting up in the blanket, his sandy blonde hair almost completely covering his eyes .

"Sorry, I thought I'd let you sleep a little longer." Alexei smirked. With a loud yawn, Reggie began to stand.

"No time for that today, I'm afraid. We've got to get on the road as soon as possible." Reggie grabbed the small satchel he brought with him and began to change his clothes. "You should finish packing as well." Looking over toward the bed, he noticed the two bags that Alexei had brought with him. "Is that one LeBlanc's bag?"

Alexei nodded. "Yes. I brought it with me after we got separated."

"Hmm…we probably won't be able to take both." He examined the bag for a moment. "Do you need anything out of it?" Alexei shook his head. "Good. We can come back later for the bag. We should only take what we need."

As Reggie finished changing his clothes, Alexei turned away to grant him some privacy. "I believe that my bag is mostly ready. My shoes are downstairs." Saying this made him realize that he had never truly unpacked in the first place. Mrs. Swinburn had provided him with clothes to wear, so there was no need to change into the clothes he brought.

"Probably for the best, then. You're ready to go at a moment's notice. How's your knee feeling?" Reggie asked as he finished putting on his jacket and tightening the strings on his bag.

Alexei looked down to observe his knee, which was now covered by his trousers. "Seems fine today. I should be good to run a few miles or so."

Smiling, Reggie looked over at him. "Let's hope it doesn't come to that. Come on, let's see if the Misses has any breakfast before we head out."

Grabbing their bags, they both headed down the stairwell. They heard Mr. Swinburn's voice coming from the parlor at the bottom of the steps.

"The weather has been holding out lately. We've had some real nice luck so far."

There was a brief period of silence and then another voice rang out from the room. It was the sound of Sergeant Blackwell.

"It's good to hear, Al. I'm sure you've been keeping the boys busy, eh Eli?"

Eli's voice sounded sad as he replied. "Sure."

Reggie turned to face Alexei. Pointing his finger towards the back of the house, Reggie directed him to turn around. He wasn't sure why Reggie wanted to avoid a conversation with the Sergeant, but he didn't seem to be in a place to argue. He assumed he wouldn't be able to say proper goodbyes either. Turning around, he made his way to the back door with Reggie behind him.

"Ah, you boys are up!" They heard the Sergeant say from behind. Turning to face him, Alexei smirked as he saw the familiar face of the man who brought him to England only a few weeks ago. "Were you not going to tell me that you were awake? I've been waiting for almost an hour for you."

Alexei hesitated a moment. "Sorry, Sergeant. I had no idea you were coming."

Shaking his head, Blackwell walked towards them. "I suppose my letter didn't make it before my arrival." Pulling at his red beard, he looked briefly at Reggie. "I don't believe we've met."

Reggie looked suspiciously at the Sergeant. "Reginald Bellion III, Aspirant of the French Army." Blackwell looked him up and down. "I've come to take Lexi to his next destination. Your assistance will no longer be required, Sergeant Blackwell."

Blackwell grimaced. "Well, you certainly know who I am." He paced for a moment in front of them. "Tell me, Reginald, who sent you?"

"That information is classified, I'm afraid." Reggie seemed to stand tall in Blackwell's presence.

Glaring at Reggie, Blackwell responded, "Classified, indeed. Someone who knows who this boy is must certainly know his worth." Reaching to his side, Blackwell pulled out a pistol and aimed it at Reggie. "Which means that I cannot allow you to continue this fruitless journey of yours." Turning back around, Blackwell noticed that Mr. Swinburn and Eli were staring at him from the parlor. "Nothing personal, Al. I must take the boy and be off." He looked back over at Reggie. "I suppose I'll have to take this one as well since he knows too much." Waving the gun in the direction of the door, Blackwell motioned for the two to head toward the front of the house.

Mr. Swinburn emerged from the parlor as they passed by. "Thomas, what are you doing?"

Blackwell looked at him briefly. "I asked you a favor, Albert. I expect you to honor that favor and ask no questions as to why." Mr. Swinburn hung his head in disappointment.

Making their way outside, Alexei felt the barrel of the gun push into his back. Someone he trusted had once again betrayed him. Clenching his fists, he attempted to hold back tears.

"Wait!" He heard Eli shout from the doorway of the house. Blackwell turned around to face him while motioning for Reggie and Alexei to get into the car. "You have to take me too."

"What are you talking about, Eli?" Blackwell said, rolling his eyes.

Eli approached them as Blackwell opened the car door. "I know who Lexi really is."

"Eli, don't do this." Alexei shouted, shaking his head in protest.

Blackwell stared Eli down for a moment. "I don't have time for such games." He turned back towards Reggie and Alexei. "Get in the car you two!" Reggie climbed into the back as Alexei sat in the front passenger seat.

By now, Eli had created enough distance between him and his father that Mr. Swinburn couldn't hear his next words. "His name is Alexei Romanov, the crown prince of Russia," Eli said bluntly as Blackwell turned back around towards him. "He escaped, fleeing to France and then to Great Britain. His whole family was brutally murdered by Russian radicals. He..."

"Enough!" Blackwell interjected. Alexei looked back up at the house, noticing Mr. Swinburn staring off in amazement. "I'm very sorry, Al." He looked back at Eli. "Idiot! In the car with the others." He motioned for Eli to join Alexei and Reggie, and he did.

Alexei stared at Eli as he entered the back of the car. "Why did you do that, Eli? You could have not said anything, and you would have been safe."

"But you wouldn't have been, Lexi. If we don't protect each other, then what's the point?" Eli climbed into the seat next to Reggie as Blackwell slammed the door shut.

Reggie looked over at Eli and said, "Although it was a dumb move, I admire your courage." He looked out the window as Blackwell approached the driver's door. "Let us hope it is not in vain."

Starting the car with the hand crank in front of the car, Blackwell kept a close eye on the three boys inside. Once the engine began to roar, Blackwell climbed into the driver seat and slammed the door, beginning to drive down the long driveway. "I came for one, and I ended up getting three. Must be my lucky day." He shook his head as he looked at the three young men in the car with him. "Reginald, you must have been sent by LeBlanc. It's too bad the soldiers couldn't finish the job in Paris when they had the chance."

Reggie looked up, surprised at what Blackwell had just said and asked, "Aren't you and LeBlanc meant to be friends?"

Blackwell scoffed. "Everyone has a price, Reginald. Don't forget that."

Alexei looked over at him. "So, you're going to kill me then? Along with my friends?"

Straightening his back in the seat, Blackwell focused on the road. "Your friends, yes. I have no choice there. I didn't want to do that around Al. The poor man has been through enough." He focused his attention back on Alexei. "As for you, I'm returning you to the Bolshevik regime to do with you as they see fit."

"They will kill me, just as they did my family. You know this." Alexei tensed up in his seat.

"Perhaps. But that is not my place to say. My duty is to make sure you are safely returned to the Russians, where you'll be brought back to your fatherland."

"Motherland." Alexei interrupted. "We do not refer to home as the 'fatherland'."

"It matters not." Blackwell waved his hand in the air. "Besides, the Bolsheviks have a wide scope looking out for you. I wouldn't be surprised if Reggie was also a spy."

"Va te faire foutre." Reggie said, glaring at Blackwell.

"Hmph." Blackwell scoffed again, continuing to drive into the city. "It doesn't matter really. Once we get into the city, I'll dispose of the two of you and deliver the ex-crown prince back to his rightful owners."

Eli was growing angry. "Lexi doesn't belong to anyone."

"You see, that's where you're wrong. He's a prisoner of the Russian people. His family has been tried and convicted, and they must suffer their punishment." He looked over at Alexei. "All of them."

Alexei shook his head. "What happened to you, Sergeant? In a month's time, you went from someone who saved me from the same regime you are now delivering me to."

Reggie interrupted, "Money, Lexi. It's always about money."

Blackwell just smiled in response.

29

Before long, they were pulling into an alleyway on the outskirts of a desolate part of London. Around him, Alexei could see lots of people in torn, dirty clothing walking the streets. The alley was covered in grey and black. The buildings were coated in soot from the chimneys above, and the cobblestone road seemed to continue toward infinite darkness.

Alexei glanced into the back seat, noticing Reggie staring out of the window, seemingly pondering what his next move would be. Eli hung his head, wondering if he'd made the right choice. For a moment, Eli looked up and their eyes met. Alexei could see the worry in his eyes as they glanced at each other briefly before Eli darted his gaze out the window.

Suddenly, the car came to a stop. Alexei looked around, seeing they were halfway into an alley, with not another person near them.

Blackwell opened his door and proceeded to get out of the car. "All right." Blackwell took his gun and waved it toward the back at Reggie and Eli. "You two, out!"

Eli hesitated for a moment, sharing a quick glance with Alexei before moving towards the door. Reggie followed suit behind him.

Blackwell looked at Alexei. "You stay here. Don't move or I'll take care of you myself. You hear?" Alexei nodded in compliance.

Alexei watched as his two friends were led deeper into the alleyway, Blackwell using his gun to direct them. He sat there, contemplating what he could do to get out of the mess. He feared for Reggie and Eli, and he knew he couldn't let them be killed, but he wasn't sure how to help. Looking out the back window, he watched as Blackwell lined Eli and Reggie against one of the walls covered in soot, still pointing his gun in their direction.

Attempting to hear their conversation, Alexei opened his door slightly, just enough to hear what was going on.

"You'll never get away with this, Blackwell." Reggie stated. Alexei could feel his anger from his seat in the car. "You are no longer an ally to the war. Once Britain finds out that you are a traitor, they will see you executed."

Blackwell laughed. "If Britain finds out, I will have fled the country and be safely guarded as a refugee in Germany by that time. Don't look so disappointed, though. Your deaths are merely coincidental to the fact that you know who that boy is. All of this could have been avoided if you would have just stayed out of the way. Especially you, Eli. I watched you grow up, and now..."

There was a brief pause before Eli spoke. "Everything you do is a choice, Thomas. This is the path you've chosen, and I hope that one day you'll see that you were wrong."

Alexei looked around inside the car. He needed to find something to help Eli and Reggie.

"If I am wrong, I will have the money to not care. If I am right, I will also have the money to not care. The boy shall return to a Russian grave, where he belongs." Blackwell's voice became harsh in tone.

Reaching around the floor, Alexei grabbed an object from underneath the seat. It was a wrench.

Reggie spoke again, "A penny for a country. A franc for a war. A noble coward, you are."

Alexei firmly gripped the wrench in his right hand.

"Shut up! We will see who is noble!" Blackwell shouted as he raised his gun toward Reggie.

A crash resounded in the alley as Alexei thrust the wrench into the car's windshield, shattering it into pieces. Blackwell's attention was quickly pulled to the front of the alley where the vehicle sat.

"What the hell?" Blackwell said. Before he could react, Reggie rushed toward the Sergeant, pushing him up against the wall and pinning his arm with the gun in the air.

Fully opening the car door, Alexei grabbed his bag and exited the vehicle.

Reggie shouted from down the alley. "Eli! Lexi! Get out of here!" With that, Eli came sprinting toward Alexei.

As Eli got closer, he heard him ask, "Can you run?"

Alexei nodded as Eli grabbed him by the hand, ushering him down the rest of the alley. Behind them they heard Reggie and Blackwell still struggling for the firearm. Alexei noticed that Blackwell was attempting to kick Reggie off him, but Reggie was pushing back in retaliation.

"Come on!" Eli shouted, pulling on Alexei, as he wondered what would happen next. His brain kept thinking of possible scenarios that could happen in the next few minutes but couldn't tell if any of them were feasible enough to see all of them living through this, including the Sergeant.

Rounding the corner of the alley, Alexei and Eli looked up and down the street, looking for the safest path. To their left, there were a few buildings with tiny crowds of people. To their right, more buildings, but seemingly void of people.

A gunshot came from the alley, and the two just stared at each other for a moment, seemingly fearing the worst. They looked over as they watched people on the street react, trying to find the source of the sound as if looking for a car that had just backfired.

Eli noticed a set of stone steps on the right. "Quick! Over here!" Still grabbing onto Alexei's hand, he pulled him behind the steps to hide. They both kept their eyes on the alley, ready to run if they saw Blackwell turn the corner.

In a flash, Reggie appeared in the street, looking both ways for the two of them.

Alexei stood up. "Reggie!" He shouted as Reggie immediately turned toward them and ran.

Alexei was fascinated at how quickly he moved. Upon reaching them, he didn't waste any time. "This way!" he said, pointing further down the road. "If we continue down this path, the safe house shouldn't be too far from here."

The three young men darted off, Reggie leading the way down the road.

30

Rounding the corner, Alexei, Reggie, and Eli darted through the streets of London, attempting to find the safe house that Reggie had been referring to. People watched as they darted by, unknowing of who they were, but continuing their day as if they hadn't even seen them. The buildings began to look cleaner as they reached the end of a road, a distinct separation from those that could afford to have the outside of their houses cleaned and those that couldn't.

Reggie looked both ways before turning left and said, "We shouldn't be too far." They slowed to a walk, allowing Reggie to lead.

Checking his surroundings, there seemed to be more people in the area, most were well-dressed in their petticoats and suit jackets. The distinction between the poor and the rich seemed to be made very clear in London, and Alexei wondered what anyone in the middle class would have worn.

Making their way down the road, Alexei noticed a signpost reading the name of the street, 'Portobello Road'.

Eli also took notice as he spoke up. "From what I've heard, there's often a huge market on this road. The war has put a damper on a lot of those activities though, for fear of bombings."

Alexei looked up and down the road as more people began shuffling their way into the street. "I pray there may be some normalcy soon."

"Ey, you two! Keep up with me, will you?" Reggie shouted at them as Alexei realized they were a few paces behind. Taking a few long strides, their pace quickened to catch up with him. "Blackwell may still be on our tail. We must keep an eye out."

Eli glared at him. "You mean you didn't kill him?"

Surprised, Reggie responded. "Why would I kill him? There's no honor in murder, remember that."

"But he was going to kill us." Eli proclaimed.

Reggie's pace seemed to slow for a moment. "You don't repay death with death. It only leads to more turmoil."

Alexei chimed in. "Reggie's right, Eli."

"So, you wouldn't take the lives of those that took your family's lives?" Eli interjected, staring at Alexei, his face now looking concerned.

"I..." Alexei hesitated. "I cannot say."

Reggie turned around. "Eli, that's enough. This is not the time to be asking those questions. We're here." Moving in the direction of a lone white house on the street surrounded by row buildings, the three moved closer with the crowd of people.

"I'm sorry, Lexi." Eli said softly.

Shaking his head, Alexei responded. "Do not worry. It is all right." He put a hand on Eli's shoulder.

Suddenly, Reggie stopped, causing Eli and Alexei to almost bump into him. The people around them continued to walk, making Alexei feel like an obstruction in the flow of traffic.

Eli lightly shoved Reggie in response, pushing himself backwards. "Hey, what's the big idea?"

"Something's not right." Reggie said quickly. He looked around for a moment before noticing a car parked on the other side of the street. "Quick, let's get behind that car. Careful to not be spotted." They moved with the flow of people, cutting diagonally to get across the street to the car that was sitting by itself. Reggie crouched down behind it and the other two followed suit.

Alexei looked over at Reggie, who was peering from around the car towards the house. "What's wrong?"

"The guards are positioned incorrectly." Reggie took his hand and placed it behind his back. Alexei watched as his fingers slowly came out one by one until he reached four. "Four guards stationed in the front, one on each side. This post only requires two guards for the front, with one on each side. Two of the guards must be imposters." He continued to look over the car. "But which ones?"

"Does it really matter?" Eli interjected. "If there are two guards that are Russian soldiers, then the whole safe house is most likely compromised."

Reggie looked Eli over, then looked back towards the safe house.

Alexei placed a hand on Reggie's shoulder. "I'm afraid that Eli is right, Reggie."

"I know." Reggie murmured under his breath, not wanting to admit that Eli had a point.

Eli grew impatient. "Is there anywhere else we can go?"

Alexei thought for a moment. "What if we went back to the Swinburn's house? We can at least regroup and figure out our next move."

Reggie shook his head in defiance. "There's no time for that."

The silence among the three of them seemed to last minutes before Alexei finally chimed in. "What if we just go to the palace?"

Reggie looked at him confused. "Buckingham Palace?"

"Yes." Alexei felt that it was a better option, if not the only one, at this point. "I know that Blackwell didn't even try to get me a meeting with the king, but I am sure that I can prove who I am. I'm the only one who knows everything about my own family, right? Surely, they'd have to let me in at some point."

Letting himself think, Reggie looked at Alexei. "The palace has to be on the other side of town."

"So, what are we waiting for?" Eli interjected again.

Turning back to Alexei, Reggie took a deep breath and nodded. "Okay, let's go."

Rising from behind the car, the three began to walk in the opposite direction of the safe house. Crowds of people still rushed by, causing Alexei to grab onto Eli's shirtsleeve to stay close. Reggie still maintained the lead among the three, leading them further down the road.

"Hey! Stop!" Alexei heard a man's voice yell from behind him.

"We've got trouble! Run!" Reggie yelled, sprinting toward another section of the street. Looping around a bend, they made their way down an even more crowded area, making it harder to push through the hordes of people.

"Somebody stop those three boys!" The same man's voice reverberated into Alexei's ears as they darted through the crowd. He didn't have time to turn around, but he wanted desperately to see the face of the man who was chasing them.

Turning another corner, Reggie grabbed Eli's arm and pulled him along, causing Alexei to get pulled as well, still hanging onto his sleeve.

"Keep going!" Reggie said, motioning for the two to continue without him.

Alexei protested. "What? No!"

"Trust me, Lexi. You must get to a safe place. Get to the palace. Go and..." Before Reggie could finish his sentence, a blow from a fist knocked him to the ground.

"Reggie!" Alexei's attention turned toward the guard who was looking at him, now with a gun pointed directly at his chest.

Alexei threw his hands in the air as another guard rounded the corner. The two men looked almost identical as if they were twins. "You, you're coming with us!" The other guard said, in a thick Russian accent.

In an instant, Reggie came out of nowhere and jumped on the back of the first guard, causing the second guard to stumble and dart toward Reggie. Eli jumped in and attempted to push the guard out of the way. With a huge thrust, the guard went flailing into the wall, dropping the pistol he was holding onto the ground. Scrambling to grab the gun, Eli rushed the other guard, causing him to flinch before attempting again to reach for the pistol, but Eli made it first, grabbing it and pointing at the guard. The second guard slowly put his hands above his head as he stood, waiting for Eli to make his next move.

The first guard spun Reggie around on his back as Reggie tried to keep the gun from pointing at Alexei, Eli, or himself. "Get off of me!" With a thrust, the guard threw Reggie over him, causing him to land on his back. "We must reclaim the prisoner, no matter the cost." He pointed his gun at Reggie who was still recovering from the guards throw, attempting to roll over onto his knees.

A gunshot fired, and Alexei screamed. "No!"

Time seemed to move slowly for those next few moments. Looking at Eli, his gun was still pointed at the second guard who had his hands in the air, seemingly giving up. Reggie lay still on the ground, holding his pose. The first guard held still for a moment, then reacted, dropping the gun, and falling to the ground, grabbing at the gunshot wound in his neck. Time resumed as the guard laid there motionless, becoming surrounded in a pool of his own blood.

"Is everyone all right?" A familiar voice said from Alexei's left. Turning his head, he saw Officer Jean-Pierre Dupont, from the French Army in Nice, appearing out of thin air, dressed in his finely pressed officer's uniform.

Alexei looked around again. "I think so." He rushed over to help Reggie, allowing him to wrap his arm around his shoulders to stand.

"We would have been fine without your help, Dupont." Reggie brushed off his trousers, turning around to see that Eli was still pointing his gun at the second guard.

Dupont also turned his attention toward the second guard. "Well, what do we do about this one?" His gun was raised towards the second guard.

The defenseless man shook his head. "Please! I won't say anything! I'll forget this even happened! Please!"

Turning his attention toward Reggie, Dupont asked. "What do you think?" Reggie just gave a half smile, causing Dupont to reflect Reggie's smile and turn back to the guard. "Fair enough." Raising the barrel of the gun quickly, he approached and brought it down sideways into the temple of the guard's head, causing him to fall to the ground. "That should do."

"What are you doing here?" Reggie asked as he picked up the gun from the first guard and slipped it into the back of his trousers.

"Someone told me that you needed help. I journeyed to London at the request of General LeBlanc himself. I was in the safe house when I heard those guards yell after you, which is why I came running." Dupont slid his weapon back into its holster.

"So, the house is safe?" Eli asked, waving the gun around loosely, causing Reggie to grab it, stabilizing his grip. Alexei was sure that Eli couldn't have known who Dupont was but seeing that Reggie trusted him must have given Eli enough sense to trust him as well.

Dupont focused his attention on Eli as Alexei walked over to speak. "I wouldn't go that far. Now that the Russian soldiers know where it is, we will have to take you to another safe house." He looked over at Alexei, who appeared stunned. "Don't think that we have just one safe location in such a large city." Patting Reggie on the back, he continued. "Now, is everyone ready? I don't want to be around when this man wakes up from his nap."

31

The other safe house was a twenty-minute walk from where they left the two Russian soldiers on the side of the road, one unconscious and one most certainly dead. The house fit perfectly into its surroundings, with brick walls lining up the side with six windows placed strategically between the first and second floors of the home. The solid wood door looked very heavy as Alexei stared at it, wondering if it would even budge if he tried to open it by himself.

Leading the way, Dupont ushered them up the stoop to the front door. Placing his hand near the door, Alexei watched as Dupont knocked three times in succession, then twice, three more times, followed by a single knock.

"All aboard, yo ho, all aboard, ho." Reggie sang quietly under his breath as if chanting a tune in sync with Dupont's knocking. Dupont smiled when he heard Reggie's chant.

Suddenly, the door opened, revealing a plain-dressed young man with shaggy brown hair staring back at them.

"Dupont. Qu'est-ce que vous faites ici?" The young man

said, asking why Dupont was there.

Dupont spoke so fast in his native language that Alexei couldn't figure out what he was saying in response to the man. But afterward, he opened the door and allowed the four men inside, ushering them in quickly.

The interior of the house appeared old and decrepit, almost as if it hadn't been lived in for years. Everything on the first floor seemed visible from the front entrance. The kitchen stood off to the right with a small dining room attached. To the left was a sitting area with stairs that led to the upper floor. In front of them was an open space with a washroom in the back. A table sat in the middle of the open space with a tablecloth decorated with fleur-de-lis all around it.

"We should be safe here until we can figure out what to do next." Reggie responded, moving further into the house.

Eli looked around, taking in the surroundings. "How do we know that the Bolsheviks aren't aware of this house if they knew about the other one?"

Reggie's stance seemed to stiffen. "We'll have to go on good faith that they don't."

Dupont removed his hat, focusing his attention on Alexei. "I do not believe you should have any trouble here, your royal highness. The soldiers appeared to be an isolated incident, otherwise, we would have seen more than two. Our guards didn't even seem aware that they were standing there."

"Until that one soldier wakes up and goes back to tell everyone else where we are." Eli snapped back at Dupont. "You shouldn't have let him live."

Alexei stared at Eli intensely, and said, "It's senseless to take a life if it isn't necessary."

Eli shook his head. "Lexi, these soldiers are after you. I don't understand why you aren't doing everything you can to protect yourself. And even more, why aren't we?"

"So, why didn't you shoot him then?" Dupont said accusingly at Eli, which reminded Alexei of his scolding of Ivan back at the military palace in Nice. "You had a gun pointed right at him and a chance to finish him off." Suddenly, Eli seemed to relax, allowing his shoulders to slump. "Perhaps you knew at the time that it wasn't the best course of action to take." Eli hung his head as Dupont approached him and placed a hand on his shoulder. "A true soldier knows when it's time to shoot or scurry. If you intend to accompany his royal highness, you must know when to act appropriately."

Alexei looked over at Eli again. "We learn these things as a team, Eli. Don't forget, we are on this journey together now." He turned his attention to Dupont. "General Dupont, I thank you for your assistance today. You've been a valuable asset. I don't know where we would be without your aid."

"Of course, your royal highness." Bowing his head, Dupont glanced at Reggie before excusing himself.

Reggie gave Eli a glance and a smirk before turning his attention toward Alexei. "Come on, Lexi. Let's get you settled upstairs for now. We can talk more later." Ushering Alexei upstairs, Eli followed close behind.

At the top of the steps, four rooms branched off from the main hall. One of the doors was shut, which Alexei assumed belonged to the young man who let them in. The other three rooms stood wide open, each with a bed and a nightstand. Reggie motioned for Alexei to take his pick of a room. They all seemed to be the same size, so he chose the far-right corner room and made his way down the hall.

Entering the room, he noticed the window on the far side looking out onto a small park with a few benches and lots of people walking, some with their dogs. He smiled at the thought of being able to walk around the park someday, without fear that someone might be out to get him. He placed his bag down on the bed and sat down for a moment, taking a deep breath to collect his thoughts.

A little over a month had passed since he and his family were taken into a dark basement in the middle of the night. Since his family was murdered right in front of him. Since he was rescued by an old man and his wife, who were gracious enough to see him safely out of Russia, simply because they believed in him and his family.

His father had abdicated the throne over six months ago, but chaos still reigned in the motherland. The war of the world may have been close to its final curtain, but the battle in his home remained steady, the people and the Bolsheviks consistently pushing back against one another. He wondered if order would ever be established again, or if the throne would forever be shrouded in chaos.

A knock at his door brought Alexei back to reality. Turning his head, he noticed Eli standing in the doorway.

"Can I come in?" Eli asked, his tone seemed timid.

Alexei nodded. "Of course." Waving his hand, he motioned for him to enter and sit next to him, to which Eli complied.

"Lexi..." Eli started nervously. "I'm sorry for what I said earlier, about your family. It was wrong and I should have thought about what I said before I said it. Forgive me."

"Eli, you have nothing to apologize for." Alexei placed his hand on Eli's shoulder. "If anything, I should be the one apologizing to you."

Eli looked at him confusingly. "What for?"

"For telling you who I really was. It is my fault that you and Reggie are in this mess in the first place." Alexei looked down at the floor, unsure of whether to feel ashamed.

"Lexi..." Eli tried to get his attention. "If I didn't want to be by your side, I wouldn't have said anything in the first place." Alexei lifted his head, allowing his eyes to meet Eli's. "The only reason I told Thomas that I knew about you was because I believed in you, and I still do. You've come so far and have endured so much pain. You deserve to have people standing beside you through it all."

Alexei smiled in response.

"Precisely." Reggie's voice came from the doorway. "If we didn't want to be here, Lexi, we wouldn't be. We are here because we have faith in you. You're practically family now." Entering the room, Reggie moved towards the two sitting on the bed.

"Besides..." Reaching into his pocket, he pulled out the red jewel that Alexei had given him. "We have a promise to keep, no?"

Seeing the red jewel, Eli reached into his pocket, pulling out his green jewel.

Alexei couldn't contain his smile as Reggie and Eli looked at him, each holding on to their jewel. "Thank you both. I truly don't know what I would do without you."

Eli clutched his jewel tightly. "This journey is far from over, Lexi." Looking at him, Alexei could tell that he was staring at his chest. Remembering the ruble with his father's face on it, Alexei grabbed at the coin around his neck. "It's up to you to figure out what is next."

Smiling, Alexei knew what Eli meant by that. Thinking about his family and everything that had happened over the last couple of years, it was time to take this journey into its next chapter. His sisters had taken great strides to ensure his safety, it would be reckless to let them down, even in death.

"The throne might not be possible to recover." Alexei began. "But what should be done are the proper reparations to restore the family line to decency and condemn a regime that sought out the murder of a member of the royal family." He looked at Reggie and Eli, as they stared back at him. "My father's life alone was too much, not to mention that of my mother and sisters. The only way this world can move forward is for the world to know the truth. That the Bolshevik regime, led by Vladimir Lenin and Leon Trotsky, murdered the Romanov family in cold blood, except for the one who got away. One who will stand up against the hatred and not be afraid any longer to speak his truth."

Reggie and Eli looked at each other for a moment, inspired by Alexei's speech.

Reggie let out a faint cough before speaking. "So does that mean..."

Alexei finished his sentence, feeling like he knew what Reggie was going to say next. "Yes." He nodded. "We are going to find a way, no matter what, to get into Buckingham Palace, so that I may speak with Cousin George myself and prepare a proper declaration to the world's stage." He turned to look out the window. "The world will know that Alexei Nikolaevich, Tsarevich of Russia, is alive, and has quite a story to tell."

EPILOGUE

Greagor Crowther had just finished writing his final notes for the evening, tucking them away into a folder and sliding it back into a drawer of his desk. The last month had been a whirlwind of puzzles and confusion, doubting if the war outside the four walls of his house was even real. The revelations that had taken place before his eyes seemed to finally start falling into place. He had noticed Russian soldiers parading around London just the other day. They wouldn't be present if the rumors were not indeed true.

A knock at the door prompted Crowther to look up from his desk, staring at the door where the sound had originated. He wasn't quite sure how long he'd been seated in his office, a few hours at least. "Yes?" His voice lingered with a sense of eeriness but was backed by a confident tone.

The door opened, revealing a sharply dressed man holding a duster in his hand. "Excuse me, Lord Crowther, someone is here to see you."

It was the man he had been expecting. "Show him in."

Crowther motioned for the butler to retrieve him, and he complied, shutting the door, and leaving him alone again in the office.

Crowther was visited by this man every few days for a little over a month now, each time growing closer and closer to the meaning of his visits. At first, the man had been friendly, merely looking for a chat about local politics, the lack of confidence in the Prime Minister, or whatnot. Slowly, their conversations began to grow more specific, asking about the King's thoughts on the civil war in Russia. Crowther paid no mind to the man at first, as they seemed like mere ramblings of someone with nothing better to do. However, the more the man spoke, the more intrigued Crowther became. Suddenly, casual conversations divulged into conspiracy theories of the Romanov family being murdered, and there was speculation of a survivor. Russia had been quiet ever since the admittance of the Tsar's execution, so it was easy to speculate what could have happened to the rest of the family.

Pushing his slick black hair out of his face, Crowther arched his back to stretch for a moment. As a man in his mid-forties, he tried not to sit so long as it made getting up even harder. He twisted his body to one side, then the other, attempting to crack his bones into a comfortable state.

The man who would be entering any moment had had a profound impact on him over the last few days. The theories and stories seemed to spiral until one thing found its way into his possession.

Looking down at the desk, Crowther moved his hand toward the drawer on the far left. Gripping the handle and pulling it toward him, he then heard another knock at the door.

"Come." Crowther said as the door opened, and the man began to enter. "I trust you have news for me?"

The man closed the door behind him. "Not as good of news as we had hoped."

"That is...unfortunate." Crowther said, looking back down, staring at the yellow jewel given to him by the man the day before. Grabbing the jewel in his hand, he pulled it out of the drawer and clasped it tightly. "Please explain, Sergeant Blackwell."

Blackwell took a deep breath before taking another step toward Crowther. "I went to get the boy to bring him here, but there was already someone else, a Frenchman, who had come to take him first. I took them at gunpoint to an alley on the outskirts, but I was overtaken by the Frenchman, and they ran off before I could get back on my feet."

Crowther moved the yellow jewel around in between his fingers while pacing back and forth in front of the desk. "So, they got away?"

"I'm afraid so." Blackwell took off his hat. "But they must still be somewhere in the city. There's no way that they could escape on foot, and the trains are currently down."

"Perhaps..." Crowther looked down at the jewel. "Who else knows about this boy?"

Blackwell hesitated for a moment. "The...son...of the family that I took him to. He's the only one though, the rest of the family do not know anything."

Crowther lifted his brow. "How can we be sure?"

"I can assure you that they do not know, nor will they." Blackwell moved a few steps towards him.

"And fail me again?" Crowther continued staring at the jewel, paying no attention to Blackwell. "No, this is something that my own men will deal with now." He turned around, facing away from Blackwell.

"Please, Lord Crowther. They are ignorant to this situation." Blackwell seemed to plead.

"You really should have thought of all this before you agreed to aid in our cause, Sergeant." Crowther said, as he continued walking away from Blackwell back towards his desk. "Of course, by not fulfilling your duty, there is no compensation for you." Whipping his head, he hissed. "So, what are you still doing here?"

Blackwell backed up slowly towards the door, nodding as

he grabbed the doorknob, letting himself out quickly.

Crowther rang the bell, calling for the butler.

A few moments went by until the door opened again.

"Yes, my Lord?" The same man from earlier entered.

"Tell the men to meet in the study in one hour. We've much to discuss." Crowther turned towards the butler. "Oh, and see to it that the Sergeant is thoroughly observed. His loyalty appears shaky at best."

"Aye." The butler said before closing the door again.

Returning to his desk, he sat down before placing his elbows on the surface, still holding the yellow jewel between his fingers, gazing as the light pierced through it.

"What will you do now, little Romanov? What will you do now?"

ABOUT THE AUTHOR

D. C. Moore

Being a member of the LGBTQA+ community, D.C. Moore has found passion in writing stories that contain LGBT themes and undertones, allowing the reader to speculate and formulate tension on their own terms, as well as keeping a bit of suspense and horror in his tales to keep readers on their toes. Hailing from the Midwestern Ohio, D.C. found a passion for writing short stories and songs throughout his younger years, even winning multiple accolades and awards for both. He has a B.A. in Sociology from the University of Lynchburg (Lynchburg, VA) and a M.A. in Anthropology from Durham University (Durham, UK). He wrote his first novel, "Reunion" in 2015 and finally found the courage to publish in 2022, followed by the sequel, "Retribution", in 2023. D.C. enjoys giving his readers the ability to find themselves somewhere in the story and encourages them to reach out with their thoughts and ideas through his social media platforms.

BOOKS BY THIS AUTHOR

Reunion

As the ten-year high school reunion approaches in the quiet town of Fairborn, memories of a tragic murder/suicide still haunt the minds of the former classmates. One of their own had been accused of a heinous crime that ended in their own demise. Now, four years later, the reunion beckons them back. The twist? It's not just any reunion; it's a lock-in at a remote cabin nestled deep within the eerie woods. Most of the alumni seem reluctant to attend, given the unsettling circumstances. However, for those who brave the event, a night of unexpected reconnections, shocking revelations, and long-buried questions awaits. Is this gathering merely an opportunity for old friends to reminisce and make amends, or is there a darker, more ominous agenda lurking behind the gathering? As the night unfolds, the attendees must grapple with the uncertainty of their fate and whether the past holds secrets that refuse to stay buried.

Made in the USA
Middletown, DE
30 June 2024

56598086R00125